"You're hurting me," Lucy managed to moan

"You deserve it," Jim returned.

'Daddy!" His daughter, Maude, had rolled down the window of the car and was leaning out, yelling.

"Lord, I wish I were bigger," Lucy told him. "I'd—"

"If you were bigger I'd hit you back," he replied. "But, since you're such a tiny thing, I think I'll—"

"Daddy!" Maude interrupted.

"Don't," Lucy said weakly.

Don't was obviously not in this man's vocabulary. He moved closer, enclosed her in both arms and sealed the rest of her protests under a long, teasing kiss.

EMMA GOLDRICK describes herself as a grand-mother first and an author second. She was born and raised in Puerto Rico, where she met her husband, a career military man from Massachusetts. His postings took them all over the world, which often led to mishaps—such as the Christmas they arrived in Germany before their furniture. Emma uses the places she's been as backgrounds for her books, but just in case she runs short of settings, this prolific author and her husband are always making new travel plans.

Don't miss any of our special offers. Write to us at the following address for information on our newest releases.

Harlequin Reader Service
P.O. Box 1397, Buffalo, NY 14240
Canadian address: P.O. Box 603,
Fort Erie, Ont. L2A 5X3

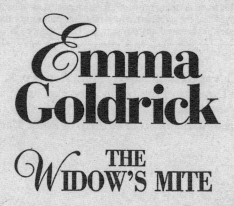

Emma Goldrick

THE WIDOW'S MITE

Harlequin Books

TORONTO • NEW YORK • LONDON
AMSTERDAM • PARIS • SYDNEY • HAMBURG
STOCKHOLM • ATHENS • TOKYO • MILAN
MADRID • WARSAW • BUDAPEST • AUCKLAND

This novel is dedicated to Mrs Anne Porter, the Doyenne of our family, who lives and does good works in the town that the Indians named Mattapoisett, The Place of Sweet Water.

Harlequin Presents first edition August 1993
ISBN 0-373-11576-8

Original hardcover edition published in 1992
by Mills & Boon Limited

THE WIDOW'S MITE

CHAPTER ONE

LUCY BORDEN swore she would never forget that morning in July. It was the day she met the Most Horrible Man in the World. Well, she met his daughter first. Lucy was sitting disconsolately on the bottom stair of her shabby front porch, staring out at the absence of traffic on Ned's Point Road, listening to the sound of the surf from behind the house, wondering what to do about *it*.

Above her head the gulls wheeled and dived and yelled at each other. The sun had reached an equitable ninety degrees Fahrenheit. A brisk sea breeze was Mattapoisett town's only salvation. It rustled up from the beach behind her house, dropped some of the salt smell on her, and then hurried across Ned's Point Road to sway the leaves of the ranks of trees that lined the road.

It. All along Ned's Point Road stretched magnificent new or refurbished estates. The Borden house, of eighteenth-century architecture, was the only one that looked as if it was about to fall down. And Lucy Borden—Lucastra, actually—had neither inheritance nor training to prevent it.

So, when the child appeared around the corner of the house and stood sturdily in front of her, Lucy pulled herself up and out of the blues and smiled. She liked children.

"Hello. My name's Maude," the child said, and extended a grubby paw. Poor little bit, Lucy thought. A lot like me when I was young. Not cute at all. A solid block of a child, built like a fire hydrant. Freckles wrestled for control of her square face. Her mousy brown hair was trimmed in a butch cut and her teeth were a straggly mix of adult and baby molars. Eight, perhaps?

She was dressed in a pair of pants that even a bag lady would refuse, along with a pink blouse that certainly came out of a Salvation Army collection box. "I'm a girl," the child added and she shifted her weight from one foot to the other.

"So am I," Lucy acknowledged gracefully as she gently shook the proffered hand. "Isn't that nice? I take it you walked up the beach?" The child nodded. "Maude what?"

"What?"

"Most people have two names. Perhaps you're Maude Somebody?"

The little girl giggled. "You're funny. Maude Somebody! My dad is a very 'portant fellow. Maude Proctor."

"Very nice," Lucy said. "A very tasty name, Proctor. Something to do with soap, I believe. Did your dad pick your first name? It's very feminine."

"I'm not sure," Maude replied in a very serious tone of voice. "Sometimes he acts like he don't like girls."

"He must have liked your mother."

"I don't have any mother. She died when I was born." So, Lucy told herself, that's what you get for being nosy, trying to subtly poke around in other people's business and you put your feet into your mouth, up to the knees. The child doesn't care to be reminded about her mother, I'll bet. And yet... "We're two alike," Lucy said softly. "My mother died when I was born, too. I never ever did see her."

The little girl sucked in her breath in sympathy, and then plumped herself down on the lowest stair. "Daddies are nice to have," she sighed. "Where's your daddy?"

"He's—not here," Lucy said. Her father had gone off to fight when she was still in teacher's college and hadn't come back. And poor Mark, too, she told herself. How could it be? They called the air guard to duty, and Dad and Mark served on the same air crew. How's that for bad luck, to lose your father and your fiancé at the same time? But that was years ago, Little Miss Gloom. Brighten up.

"But he loved you, and you loved him?" A sage nod from her little auditor. And, of course, it's true, Lucy thought.

"My dad yells at me. I really don't think he likes girls."

"Well, if your father doesn't like girls that's pretty stupid of him," Lucy judged, wondering who *he* might be. Proctor? "Is he a stupid man?"

"Him?" The child looked astonished, as if the thought had never crossed her mind. "He's the *smartest* man in the world. Or at least in Massachusetts. I'll bet you're smart too."

"No, I wouldn't say that," Lucy said gravely. "In fact, probably just the opposite. A schoolteacher doesn't make a lot of money. If I can't find another job for the summer vacation I'll be in a lot of trouble."

"Oh, but you're pretty." Said in a very firm and definitive manner, as if that were all a girl needed to succeed in the world. A judgment that would not easily be retracted. An unconditional compliment.

And what do you say to that, Lucy Borden? she asked herself. Five feet four, green eyes, one hundred and twenty pounds, plump but curved in nice proportions, with her light brown hair up in braids. Well, why look a gift horse in the mouth? "Thank you," she murmured. "But I *am* getting on, you know. I'm twenty-eight."

"That's very old," little Maude agreed solemnly as she kicked the sand with the toe of her worn shoes. "But he's a lot older 'n you." There followed a deep silence, where only the splash of the waves curtsying up to the shore and the scream of the gulls overhead actually penetrated. Lucy developed a nagging curiosity about who "he" might be, but hadn't the gumption to ask.

"Do you live around these parts?"

"Up there." Maude gestured up the beach, where a magnificent new ranch-style house graced a couple of acres, including a semicircular drive, two-space garage, and some fifteen rooms. It had been the subject of Lucy's mad curiosity for a couple of years, but as yet she had never been inside. "But in the summer it's terrible lonesome around these parts. I don't suppose...?"

"You're always welcome to come visit me," Lucy said. "Almost any time. I'm out of work again, so I'll be here most of the time. Would you like some lemonade and cookies?"

"I'm not allowed to eat between meals." The deep blue eyes stared at her as if demanding she break the rules. Lucy patted the stair beside her and rose gracefully.

"Dieting doesn't matter on Tuesdays," she offered. The child nodded sagely. There was a meeting of minds. They both knew this was Thursday, but neither was about to let a mere calendar interfere with their pleasure. "I'll get a little something."

Lucy smoothed down her green cotton skirt, tugged her orange tank top around a bit to make it more presentable, and started up the stairs. The sound of the car stopped her. A big Cadillac came rushing up Ned's Point Road past her house, the brakes squealed in torment, the engine roared as the vehicle backed up, and it wheeled into her drive as if it were conducting a police raid.

The two girls stood and watched. Maude was at the bottom of the rickety stairs, her fist crammed over her mouth, Lucy at the top with one hand still stretched out toward the front door. A little cloud of sand settled around the car, the driver's door opened, and *he* got out.

A big man, square and bulky, like his daughter, but not an ounce of fat on him. He looked as if he might top six feet rather easily. A heavy frown creased his angry face. He looked like Thor, disguised in a three-piece gray suit, about to cast a few thunderbolts.

"What the hell are you doing with my daughter?" he said in a deep bass roar that frightened the birds wheeling overhead. He was just the sort of man one could come to hate, Lucy told herself as she whipped up a little anger of her own.

"I don't allow cursing on my property," she snapped at him. "Just who are you?"

"I'm Maude's father," he roared.

"And how do I know that?" Lucy returned at the same level. "For all I can see, you might be a child snatcher. No self-respecting girl would have you for a father. Maude?"

The girl ducked her head and stubbed at the sand again, before admitting, "Yes, he's my father, but it's not my fault." A tear ran down her face. Lucy, touched to the heart, hurried back down the stairs and enveloped the child in her arms.

"No, no, dear. It's not your fault. We none of us can choose our relatives."

"Thanks a lot," the man muttered sarcastically. "Maude, get in the car."

"I'll see you again?" the child pleaded.

"Any day," Lucy replied.

"The hell you say," the man added. He slammed the car door behind his daughter and strode over to the stairs. "Now look," he said. He might have thought he was acting in moderation; his size and disposition were enough to frighten the daylights out of almost any twenty-eight-year-old woman. Lucy clenched both fists until the nails bit into her palms, and closed her eyes for good measure. But after the "Now look" he wasn't saying anything.

Cautiously she opened one eye. His eyes matched his hair, deep and murky black. But they weren't actually looking at Lucy. They were scanning the building behind her. She could almost hear him think, What a dump. And that was enough to spur her anger.

"Well, it's a home," she snapped. "We Bordens have been in this area for two centuries. We're not some Johnny-come-lately bunch of immigrants!" It wasn't true, of course. The Borden family *were* a bunch of immigrants, descended as they were from the Chases, who had come over on the *Mayflower* from the old country.

But, right or wrong, it stirred him up. His face flushed as he leaned toward her. She shifted ner-

vously up to the second step, which placed her almost
at his level.

"New England Yankee," he muttered scornfully.
"The house looks as if it were a thousand years old.
Another good wind and it'll collapse into a pile of
lumber. What with all that time and money, you'd
think you or your ancestors could have spared the time
to put a coat of paint on the damn building. It's eye-
sores like this that run down the property values of the
rest of us."

Too much, too much. Lucastra Borden felt the rage
build to explosive level. Her left hand opened and flew
in the general direction of his cheek. She closed her
eyes, not wanting to see the impact.

It was just as well. There was no impact. Inches before her palm struck, her wrist was caught up in his
massive hand, and held rigidly in place, beyond her
control.

"You're hurting me," she managed to moan.

"You deserve it," he returned.

"Daddy!" His daughter had rolled down the window of the car and was leaning out, yelling.

"Lord, I wish I were bigger," Lucy told him.
"I'd——"

"If you were bigger I'd hit you back," he replied.
"But, since you're such a tiny thing, I think I'll——"

"Daddy!" his daughter interrupted.

"Don't," Lucy said weakly.

"Don't" was obviously not in his vocabulary. He
moved closer, enclosed her with both arms, and sealed

the rest of her protests under a gentle teasing kiss. It was all warmth and moisture and music to Lucy Borden. Of course, she had been kissed a time or two in her life. Somewhat more than the average. She vaguely remembered her father cautioning her on her eighteenth birthday about both quality and quantity. But of all those boys only Mark had lit her fire, and even he hadn't had the effect of this overwhelming emotion, this punishment inflicted by—a pirate! And when, hours later, it was over and he stepped away from her Lucy felt just the slightest bit of sorrow at its ending.

It hadn't been hours later, of course. Little Maude was still yelling from inside the car, and doing her best to open the door again. The same gulls were wheeling over the house in slow motion, and Proctor was grinning at her from the bottom of the stairs.

"And let that be a lesson to you," he said. "Leave my daughter alone. It's not that you personally are such a terrible mess, but rather that your generation is a pain in my butt." At which he turned his burly back in her direction and stalked around the car to the driver's door.

Lucy worked up a little bit of bravado. "Come any time you like," she yelled at Maude. The driver looked at her over the low roof of the car and shook his finger back and forth.

"I can't let him get away with that," Lucy muttered under her breath. But what she wanted to say was not really ladylike. Besides, he might come back and punish her again. She waved to the child and muttered, "The hell you say," under her breath, then relaxed as he climbed in behind the wheel and started the engine. Above its din Lucy could hear him lecturing the little girl about wandering away to strangers.

"And what happened today?" he asked his daughter as he put a heavy foot on the accelerator.

"Happened?"

"Don't give me that sweet-innocence bit," he muttered. "Where are the men I hired to take care of the place while I'm off working?"

"Oh, them?"

"Yes, them!"

"As far as I know, they're still in the kitchen, eating," she murmured, and then braced herself, knowing her father very well. He slammed on the brakes. The rear end of the car shivered and skidded toward the roadside ditch. He managed to regain control by sheer muscle power. The car came to a stop. He reached over and tilted the child's chin back in his direction.

"Don't fight me, Maude," he said softly. "There's an epidemic going on in New England. Children from rich families are being kidnapped right and left. Don't you remember why we moved down here to Mattapoisett rather than staying in Boston? Three separate kids, one from your own school, all grabbed. Why do you think we let you run around looking like a vagabond rather than dressed up like Little Miss Rich Kid?"

"I'm sorry, Daddy. I—just forgot. I was bored. All those men want to do is eat and talk to Mrs. Winters. You shouldn't keep such a wonderful cook. I was terribly bored, so I walked down to the beach, and there was Lucy. She's a nice lady."

"That may be, but until I know more about her we don't take any chances, baby."

"And she's pretty too."

He cleared his throat, and the child said, "Well, she is."

"Perhaps," he compromised. "But beauty is as beauty does."

"Aw, please," his daughter muttered as he restarted the engine. "Where do you get all those—what do you call them?"

"Clichés."

"Yeah. Them." The child shuffled around in her chair. "And I like her lots. She's fun. She laughs all the time. And *she* likes *me*!"

"Do you say so?" her father commented wryly as he brought the car around the drive to his own front door. "Get in the house or else——"

"Or else the sky will fall?"

"Or else the sky will fall." The little girl glared at him, but her mouth was twisting back and forth. Finally she broke out into a roar of laughter and threw herself at the big man who was her father.

"So then he drove off in a huff," Lucy said. She had related the whole story. Well, everything except the kiss. There was hardly any need to embarrass herself further on *that* score. The emaciated old woman in the bed shook her head in disgust. Every Thursday afternoon Lucy went down to the Merit Nursing Home to visit Angela Moore. Angie was in her nineties, the last of her line. Up until two years ago she had lived on the Point also, until the day she had fallen down the stairs and broken her hip.

As with many old Yankee families, the several collateral branches of the Moore family had once been virile, and had amassed several fortunes between them. But gradually the blood had grown thin and the males had all died off, leaving elderly females to inherit. Until finally, out of all those inheritors, Angie Moore had been the last, and everything had come to her. The whole town knew she was wealthy beyond compare.

What the whole town did *not* know, but Lucy thought *she* did, was that Angie had always held a great affection for the horses, and in the course of her years had bet every cent she owned on nags that would have run further and faster if someone had put training wheels on them. But Angie and Lucy shared a friendship that spanned the generation gap, and kept few secrets from each other.

"Well, he must have been a terribly rude man." Angie licked her ice-cream spoon. "And do you suppose next week you could bring me some lobster rolls, love? I can't stand the institutional food in this place."

"Of course. But the last time I did the lobster upset your stomach, Angie."

"I enjoyed them just the same," the old lady insisted. "Proctor, you said?"

"That's the name the child gave me."

"And lives up on the beach next to you?"

"The very one. I've some more ice cream in my container. Want to finish it?"

"I've heard the name before," Angie said, her eyes on the further serving. "Proctor. The family is big in something. Money, I think, but I can't quite place it. It'll come to me. Does he remind you of anybody?"

"You mean, like Mark, for instance? No, he doesn't. This man is all muscle and mouth. Mark was always a quiet one. I can't possibly compare them."

"Well, for one thing, they all wear pants," Angie commented, and then cackled.

"I don't want to talk about things like that," Lucy replied in her most prim of voices. And then there was a little break. "—I've only just begun to forget."

"I'm sorry, love." The pale blue eyes seemed to bore into Lucy. "But forget." That was the moment when the floor nurse and her aide appeared, tut-tutting about the feast, and told Lucy that visiting hours were over.

"Jealous," Angie said as she waved them off, but before they went she turned to Lucy. "You're so good to me, child, that I'm going to leave you two million dollars in my will!"

They both laughed. The nurse gasped. It was a private joke. Lucy knew that the old darling hadn't a cent to her name. But, her visit over, when she stopped at the nursing station for a moment the floor nurse leaned over the counter and said, "Boy, have you got it made. Two million!"

"Yes," Lucy agreed solemnly. "Don't let it get around town, though. My creditors will be all over me." And that, she told herself as she went down to the front doors and out into the sunshine, is a true reflection from the Bible. Angie's going to leave me her widow's mite.

As she walked slowly down Barstow Street Lucy's mind was turning over at high speed. Jobless. What to do? It wasn't her fault she had lost her clerking job at the drugstore. All the little family drugstores in Massachusetts were being swallowed up by a few big chains. Only the Seaport and the Mattapoisett drugstores remained, and they had no use for Lucastra Borden's limited talents.

"But I must have *some* assets," she murmured, disregarding the queer stares of the passersby. "I like people. Is there a people-liking job available? Mostly I like children. Is there a——?" And lightning struck her. Out of a clear blue sky Lucastra Borden had a brilliant idea!

"Children!" she yelled. The old man waiting to cross Water Street turned around and stared at her. "Children," she repeated under her breath. "There are child-care centers in town, and certainly there is a pile of children who need caring for! Now what have I got that the tots' colleges don't have?'' The answer was simple, even to a meandering mind like Lucy's: she had a beach. And a Red Cross swimming certificate, along with three years of experience as a life guard during her college years.

Her beach ran along the waterline for over a hundred feet, and extended up to the back door of her house, some seventy feet or more, all beautiful clean white sand. When someone cleaned it. ''So I'll clean the beach and organize the Little People's Beach Club,'' she told herself firmly.

She was dancing in the sunshine as she walked on over to Main Street, where she had left her car parked. Half a dozen people turned to watch as she bounced down the street. They were all summer visitors, and not worth worrying about, but, being the girl she was, she spared them each a smile. Both her dimples showed.

Luckily traffic was light as she drove east on Water Street to where it joined Ned's Point Road. The narrow two-lane street was lined on both sides by trees and brush, with the more expensive houses almost hidden on her right. Occasionally there was a glimpse of the harbor, and beyond it the swells of the Atlantic Ocean. And then there was her house, she sighed as she pulled into the drive.

Assets. She had a strong back—and a weak mind? A big house. And a beach that belonged to her. Down

to the high-water mark, of course. An old Massachusetts law required that land between high and low tidal
marks be held as public property, even though the
public had no way of access except to swim in from the
sea!

Lucy's father had always shaken his head when he
spoke of his impetuous daughter, but that had been
years ago, when she was little. Orphaned at eighteen,
when her father's aircraft was shot down, she had developed like a tiny hurricane, sweeping everyone
around her up in her excitement, even as she wandered here and there without a rudder. Now, with an
idea firmly in mind, she rushed to the telephone.

"No," the receptionist at the local newspaper,
Presto Press, told her patiently, "the deadline for
ads—new ones—is ten o'clock Thursday morning.
The next issue will be delivered on Saturday. Would
you like a classified ad inserted?"

"I had thought of a full-page advertisement," Lucy
said, and then blanched as the voice on the other end
started quoting prices. "I—no, I guess I'll have a
classified," she stuttered, and dictated her little an-
nouncement.

And now there was waiting time. Planning time.
How many children could she handle? Ten, she decided. Between five and ten years old. All girls, to
avoid the problems young males brought. If I have
them just in the morning I won't have to provide
lunches. But if it rains I just can't turn them away, so
there will have to be house games and organization.

And I'll have to get the darn roof fixed. And I'll charge—Lord, I haven't any idea what I'll charge!

Worries didn't worry you unless you thought about them. Lucy Borden thrust the problem of money out of her mind, changed into her yellow bikini, found the sand rake, and went out to do battle with her neglected beach. It was amazing how much garbage an unused beach could accumulate. She raked and shoveled and filled green rubbish bags, and suddenly it was four o'clock, and her muscles ached. There was a smooth granite boulder that marked the boundary between her property and the next. With a sigh of contentment Lucy dropped the rake, stood the shovel up in the sand, and sank down onto the gray stone marker.

Her eyes wandered back down the beach. Fit for anyone's child, she decided. Pristine, sanitary——

"There's no telling what a little manual labor can do at a dump site."

The deep male voice had come from over her shoulder. Lucy jumped up and turned defensively. Proctor, with a big grin on his square face, and wearing nothing else than a pair of very short and ragged shorts. The man you could love to hate, she told herself as she mustered a glare, hoping to zap him with a Supergirl beam from her green eyes.

Unfortunately he never looked up that high. He seemed to be mesmerized by the sliding top of her old-fashioned bathing suit. Lucy's attempt to readjust the tiny patch of top only made it worse.

"Here, let me help you." He came around the rock with both hands out.

"Get back on your own property!" He stopped in mid-stride, a surprised expression on his face. Almost as if no woman had ever dared to refuse his help before, she told herself. But he did stop, his hands fell to his sides, and his sunny expression turned cloudy. Lucy managed to make a few makeshift changes in her suit, and then turned to stalk away from him.

"Hey! You there—whatever the devil your name is!"

She pivoted gently around to face him. Gently, because the bathing suit was ten years old, and Lucastra Borden had been a late bloomer. She marked that down in the back of her mind. One new bathing suit, built large enough to cover all the necessities. "You called, Mr. Proctor?"

He came striding across the property line as if he were wearing seven-league boots. She had forgotten how big he was, and in his ragged shorts he was almost entirely on view. Lucy tried to swallow; her throat was dry. Were he dressed, she could have handled him. This almost naked male animal gave her the shakes. He brought, unannounced, certain warm feelings that Lucastra was not accustomed to. Her suntanned cheeks turned blush red, outlining the freckles across her nose.

"Yeah, I called. The name is Jim. Jim Proctor." He extended a hand the size of a shovel in her direction. Almost automatically her hands dodged behind her back. He smiled, turning on some of his undeniable charm.

"What do you want, Mr. Proctor?" she stammered.

"Jim. Call me Jim." The hand remained extended in her direction. She backed off a step or two. "Look, I've got a little problem," he said.

Ordinarily Lucastra Borden, as sweet a girl as one might ask for, would have jumped on to his problem with both feet, but there was something about him that absolutely irked her. He needed to be improved, this overbearing man. And the first step in that improvement had to be to give him a good set-down. So she smothered her normal smile and said, "My heart bleeds for you, Mr. Proctor."

All the charm disappeared. "Hearts and blood I don't need." Lucy flinched. The bear was back, and growling. "What I need is a baby-sitter."

"Oh?" Her glare met his, and she was losing ground.

"Why the hell don't you buy a bathing suit that fits?" he continued. "How do you expect any red-blooded man to conduct a business conversation when you're leaking out of that——?"

"Well, really!" she interrupted indignantly. "I didn't wear it to tease your male nerves. It just happens to be the only bathing suit I own and——"

"All right, all right," he growled. "We aren't going to get anywhere, mouthing off at each other. Would you mind if we were to start all over again?"

"That wouldn't be a bad idea." Lucy made another futile gesture toward her bikini. There was no doubt about it, the man was right. Lucastra Borden had a considerable amount to show, and it was escaping its tiny net all too fulsomely. "Wait right here," she muttered and dashed for her door.

Her tatty green robe was hanging just inside the door. She slipped into it, fumble fingered, and tied the sash with extreme care. Through the camouflage of her screen door she could see him shaking his head sadly, both hands stuffed into the pockets of his shorts. From this distance he was reduced to a less threatening size. Just like a woman, that's what he's going to say, she thought. And if he does I'm going to—to—well, I would if I were bigger! With which she squared her shoulders, took four deep breaths to calm her nerves and stomach, and went back out.

"That's better," he said. "Come down here and let's talk."

"I'm not that much of a fool. I'll stay at the top of the stairs, thank you. Not after the way you talked to me this morning—Mr. Proctor." She brushed her hair back, checked the knot on her sash, and gave him a mental *défi*. She expected lightning bolts. Instead he grinned, a wide appealing grin that was almost boyish, and a lock of his hair fell down over his forehead. Lucy had the almost overpowering urge to rush down the stairs and push that lock of hair back out of his eyes, but caught herself just in time. *Damn the man.*

Her throat was drying again. She nibbled nervously at her dry lips.

He seemed to be aware of every emotion running through her, which added to the upset. "My daughter Maude." He stopped to see if he had caught her attention. He had. "My daughter Maude has this little problem," he continued. And then stopped again.

"She's a nice girl," Lucy said when the silence had stretched too long for comfort.

"Yes, she is. Independent, stubborn——"

"Lovable," Lucy contributed.

"Yes, she is," he agreed, "and that's the problem. I need somewhere she can stay for the night. I'm—entertaining a surprise visitor tonight, and I wouldn't want Maude to be caught in the line of fire."

That tiny fit of good feeling disappeared from Lucy's heart. He's entertaining female company, and wants to get his daughter out of the way? Why, that rotten——

"It's female company," he interrupted her thoughts. "I wouldn't want Maude to——"

"To know that her father is playing around?"

"I wish I could get a few words in edgewise in this conversation," he said, sighing. "Would you be willing to take Maude in tonight?"

And there you have it, Lucy thought. Right to the point. Wouldn't it be for the best if Maude was out of sight while her father ran this orgy up at the big house? What the devil do I care about him? And at the same time, why shouldn't I care about Maude? She's a good kid.

So, having rationalized some but not all of her confused feelings, she pulled herself up again. "After what you said to me this morning, now I should take your daughter in for the night?" She glared at him. He glared back.

He shrugged. "I don't know anyone else in the neighborhood."

"So that's the deal? All of a sudden I'm useful, so you'll be nice to me? I'd feel better about it if you'd yell at me."

"You are a curious female," he murmured, and took one step up. Alarm bells went off in Lucy's mind. Wild alarms. Her head buzzed.

"No," she gasped. "You—yes, Maude can stay with me. Is this female someone she might know?" She ducked both hands behind her back to hide the nervous rattling of her fingers. He took another step up.

"You'd better believe it. Lucretia Borgia."

"Who?"

"Not too well-read, are you, Miss Borden?"

"I know who Lucretia Borgia was. I'm a schoolteacher when I'm steadily employed. I'm well-read——"

"And you're damnably curious," he said, and that grin spread even wider. "It's only overnight—I hope. I'll go back up and pack her medicine bag and her clothes. It's her aunt. Her prospective mother, come to call!''

Lucy stood on her top step, her mouth half open as if a question had frozen between her tongue and lips. Jim Proctor tipped her a one-fingered salute and started back up the beach. When he came to the boundary stone he vaulted over it and began to jog toward his back door.

''And now look what a mess you're in,'' Lucy lectured herself. ''He *was* married, or he's working to *get* married.'' There was no denying the fact that a cloud of gloom had just settled in over her head. ''Of course, that doesn't mean anything to *me*. After all, he's only the man next door. Not somebody important. Why in the world shouldn't Maude see her prospective mother tonight? And he's going to bring down her medicine bag?''

The mystery was just enough to raise her spirits. She wandered back into the house, dropped into her favorite chair in the living room, and let her imagination run wild.

CHAPTER TWO

MAUDE came down the beach at about six o'clock that evening, dragging a massively tattered stuffed bear behind her. "This is fun," she called out even before she got to the house. "You don't mind if Ruprecht comes with me?" She lifted the bear's tattered arm.

"No, I don't guess I mind," Lucy said. "Providing he doesn't eat too much."

"You know," the child mused, "that's funny. Ruprecht is a stuffed bear. He never eats anything. You're *funneeey*. That's what I told my dad, only he says funny peculiar, yes, funny ha-ha, no. Why would he say something like that?"

"I can't say that I know," Lucy responded. "Men are funny creatures. Funny peculiar, that is. You've got everything you need to spend the night?"

"Everything," the girl said positively.

"No toothbrush, no nightgown?"

"I didn't have time," Maude said, looking back over her shoulder at the mansion on the hill. There was a half-frightened look on her face. "*She* came in, and I had to get out of there in a hurry. I wouldn't wanna be anywhere's near *her*."

"No, I don't suppose you would," Lucy agreed. Make a note, Miss Borden. Find out who *she* is, and why the child is afraid of her. "Come on into the house, and I'll show you where you'll sleep, and then we'll see about dinner."

Hand in hand, the pair of them danced across the cooling sand, up the stairs, and in through the back door of the house. "Nice," little Maude Proctor said as she looked around the sparsely furnished living room. "Did you know we've got fifteen rooms in our house and most all of them are empty?"

"No, I didn't know that," Lucy said. "At least you're not crowded over there."

"Only when Daddy has all those big-shot parties, then the whole place is loaded with people who want to drink and pat me on the head. I hate being patted on the head. There's one of them that likes to pinch my cheek. Him I'm gonna murder one of these days."

"Strong words," Lucy commented, and then shrugged. "Maybe he deserves it. Now, little Miss Proctor, up here on the second floor, this is your room. And the bathroom is right next door."

Maude stopped in the middle of the door. "My room? You knew I was coming? The bed's just my size. And what lovely wallpaper! It's made out of— comic strips, aren't they?"

"Important comics." Lucy was being solemn, and finding it a difficult job. "Right out of the *Boston Sunday Globe*. This used to be my bedroom when I was growing up. My dad let me decorate it any way I wanted.''

Maude, with her eyes wide open, scanned the panorama of brilliant colors, then ran across the room and bounced on the bed. And, as an afterthought, ''You don't get angry when I bounce on the bed?''

''Not this week. Next week, though, look out!''

''How about when your dad comes home?''

Lucy blinked the tears away. It had been such a long time ago since her dad had passed away. ''He won't be coming,'' she said, almost in a whisper. ''It was hard for him to live without Mother—and finally he went off to be with her.'' She sniffed back another tear. ''But that was years ago, and now there's just me.''

The girl's solemn eyes seemed too big to fit in her face. ''I'm sorry,'' she said. ''I know. It's terrible to grow up alone. Maybe we could be friends and then we'd both have someone to talk to. Or maybe——''

The moment of silence lingered between them, like a single teardrop preparing to fall down some silken cheek. ''Or maybe?'' Lucy coaxed.

The little girl's shoulders squared, and she spoke at machine-gun speed. ''Or maybe 'cause you're old enough you could be my mother, and then we would both have someone close to us, and you'll discover that I'm a very fine girl and when I grow up I could help take care of you—if you would just help take care of *me* right now!''

And so there, Lucastra Borden told herself. The whole ball of wax. And more than a little truth in it.

She was a beautiful child. Well, beauty is in the eye of the beholder, isn't it? And it might be nice to have someone for a daughter, only——

"Only I thought you already had a mother."

The child stared stiffly at her, her hands crimped up into fists, held in parallel across her chest. "No, I don't got I—I mean, I haven't got a mother. My mother died."

"But this woman who's visiting?"

"She's my aunt, and she's terrible mean. I don't know why my dad wants to marry her in the first place. He said it was 'cause I needed someone to take care of me, and so he was gonna marry my mother's sister—Aunt Eloise—only she don't like me at all, and they finally had a big quarrel two years ago, and Eloise moved away and I thought I didn't have to worry about that, only here we are, in a terrible mess, 'cause my dad says it might have been a terrible mistake on his part 'cause he can't look after me the way he ought to on account of he has to work, you know, and he says I still need a mother, and maybe he ought to try again with Eloise." At which, completely out of breath, the child collapsed on the bed and glared mournfully into the darkest corner of the room.

"Well, that *is* a big plan. I can see that," Lucy murmured. She *had* been curious. What woman wouldn't have been? But Maude Proctor was beginning to tell her more than she cared to know about the whole subject. "Maybe we hadn't better talk about your dad. I'm sure he wouldn't be pleased to hear that you had been telling tales out of school.''

"Telling what? I haven't said anything out of school!''

"It's an expression," Lucy said hastily. "It means gossiping. Now, about this room. Will this suit, do you suppose?''

"Beaut,'' the child answered. She pirouetted to examine everything. Lucy could not help but notice the gleam in the child's eye. Had the girl been fifteen years older Lucy would have called it a hunter's eye. But Maude Proctor was much too innocent for that sort of thing.

"You know what I have in my room at home?'' Maude interrupted Lucy's thought. "Nothin'! No pictures, no pretty wallpaper, no nothin'. Everything's painted brown. Even Ruprecht likes to sleep under the bed at our place, because he can't stand the color. Only—what do I call you?''

"Lucy. Or, if you want to be fashionable, Lucastra. Here, you can wear one of my old basketball shirts for a nightgown, and we have spare toothbrushes somewhere around here. What's the problem?''

"Lucastra? Wow! The shirt says 'Old Rochester Regional.' Were you a basketball star way back when?''

"Well, not *that* far back,'' Lucy commented. "But no, I wasn't exactly a star. Not at my height. But my boyfriend at that time, *he* was. And now what's the matter?''

"Everything's fine, only—will you be—is your room close by? Sometimes in the night-time I—walk in my sleep, and——"

"Right this way, princess." With a sweeping bow Lucy indicated the open door of the bathroom, and led her little guest through and out of the other door. "And this is where I hide in the nighttime."

"Oh!" Maude's eyes lit up again. "But you don't have no pictures."

"Of course not," Lucy said, chuckling. "I'm a big girl now. I get to do all this." Her hand gestured toward the gold and willow paper, the neat dimity curtains, the utilitarian desk that stood in one corner. The table and the Singer sewing machine that occupied the other. "And when I get tired of this I change it!"

"And you wouldn't—mind if I come——?"

"Visitors are always welcome." Lucy put out one hand toward Maude's shoulder. The child came to the hand, was enveloped by it, and pressed against her hip, where she seemed to cuddle in the warmth and the softness.

"I wish," the little girl muttered, "I *really* wish I had a mother like you."

"Ah, but don't forget, I'm pretty old," Lucy said softly. "And then we would have to get your father involved, and that could be an extremely difficult operation."

"I don't understand why you don't like my dad. He's a great fellow. Everybody loves him, 'specially me." A pause for further thought. "Well, not every day, you understand. Sometimes my dad can be a real turkey."

"Yes," Lucy responded, and fished around for a statement that would not hurt the child. "I guess different people like different things. Come on, love. Wash, and let's go downstairs. I'm not sure what we can make for supper."

By unanimous decision they had hamburgers. Burgers, with a few baked beans on the side, and not a sign of green vegetables, upon which Maude commented thankfully.

"Well, now, that's only because it's a special day," Lucy insisted. "If you planned to live here forever you'd find we have green vegetables at least six times a week. Principally broccoli."

"Ugh! I'm glad I came on the right day. Even the president don't like——"

"Doesn't like," Lucy interrupted.

"Yeah. Doesn't like broccoli."

"But he has to pay a penalty," Lucy said solemnly. "He has to live in Washington, and they don't ever let him loose to live in Mattapoisett."

"I don't know if that's punishment or not," Maude said, sighing. "I've only lived in Mattapoisett for a little while, myself. C'mon, I'll help with the dishes."

The work went quickly, but even at that it was eight o'clock before they were finished. The long summer twilight was setting in. "Come on," Lucy challenged, "let's go sit on the back porch and watch the tide come in."

"That doesn't sound very lively," Maude commented gloomily, and then she giggled. But she came anyway. There was a moon, low in the east, almost full. The wind was kicking up a spray of dark waves in the outer harbor. The moonlight cast a silver path straight across the water, dancing almost up onto the Borden beach. From the house on the hill beyond them came the distance-muted roar of the party.

"They start early," Lucy commented as she tucked the ends of her windblown hair behind her ears.

"Yeah, and end late," Maude said. The little girl scooted over on the top step, until she was tucked against Lucy's hip. "And in between they lie and drink and smoke and tell dirty stories." Her face brightened. "Did you ever hear the story about——?"

"No," Lucy snapped. "And I don't want to."

"But I was only——" Whatever it was she was "only," it came to a screeching halt. The party next door had exploded out of the house and on to the beach. Three or four couples were chasing each other around in wide circles, yelling their hearts out. The theme of the game was hard to determine in the moonlight, but somehow or another it involved shedding clothes as the circle gradually swung in the direction of the Borden house.

"Maude, I think it's your bedtime," Lucy said as she started to get up.

"No, it ain't," the girl replied bleakly. "You wanted to know my family? Just stand there and watch for a while."

The racing couples had given up the circle. Two pairs of them had spread blankets and collapsed on the sand, And I hope they're not doing what I think they're doing, Lucy thought as she reached down for Maude's hand. The child was shivering, although the night was warm. The last couple still had breath left. The woman in front flanked the rock that was the property line and made straight for the porch and the watching couple. The man behind her evidently had not been in Olympic training. When he came to the rock he collapsed against it, gave an inane sort of laugh, and passed out.

The woman came plunging down toward the house, her mouth open and gasping, her feet digging into the sand as if she were a long-distance runner. There was a vague sort of smile on her face. Maude moved closer to Lucy, holding on to her with both hands.

The racing woman almost made her goal, but a piece of driftwood intervened. She tripped, slid on the sand on her knees, and then sank back on her haunches, gasping for breath. Maude did her best to hide behind Lucy. The child was almost crying, a dry sort of sob that shook her sturdy little body.

"Why, Maudie," the racer said. "What a surprise. I thought you were upstairs in bed. And who is this— little wren?"

"Go in the house, Maude," Lucy ordered brusquely, and then helped the child along with a gentle push.

The woman rose to her knees, and then used the porch rail to help her to her feet. "Well, aren't we dictatorial?" she said sweetly. "I know who you are. James keeps talking about you. Isn't that something? I've come all the way down here to marry him—to do him a favor, mind you—and all he keeps talking about is Little Lucy who lives next door! My name's Eloise, by the way.

"Look at me, my teeth are chattering," the blonde added.

"I shouldn't be surprised." Lucy knew that she was not the world's foremost prude, but *this* was too much. There was a worn bath towel hanging over the end of the porch rail. She pulled it off in one angry gesture and threw it at the woman. "Cover yourself," she snapped.

Eloise caught the edge of the towel, swirled it around her like a matador's cape, and let it drop on to the sand. "It smells," she complained.

"The horse didn't mind," Lucy snapped. "Cover yourself. We don't stand on much ceremony around here, but—standing naked in front of that little girl... why, somebody ought to horsewhip you!"

"Nude, not naked," the blonde responded as she drew the towel around her and hiccuped. "There's a difference. Naked is sexy—nude is artistic. Do you have a drink handy?"

"Not a chance. Get off my property," Lucy snarled. The other woman, taller, more robust, took one look at the tiny woman moving in her direction, and decided that retreat would be the better part of valor. She gave one high, harsh shriek, and ran as if the devil were behind her. But he wasn't. Her particular devil was in front of her. As Eloise made it past the boundary rock another figure loomed out of the dark and snatched her up. "What in the Lord's good name are you playing at?" the husky male voice demanded.

Lucy tried to close her ears but failed. "I was racing on the beach," Eloise was saying, so sweetly as to turn Lucy's stomach. "And I met that lovely little neighbor of yours. She was kind enough to loan me this towel. Isn't that nice?"

"Nice," he agreed as he urged her up the beach with one hand around her shoulders. His moment of anger had fled, evidently.

"And I saw Maude for a moment," the blonde chattered on. "Did you send her away for the night? You shouldn't have done that. I would have loved to take care of her."

And at that point, filled with sweetness and light, the conversation faded out of range. Him, Lucy told herself as she stopped and froze in place. Proctor.

The moon was skipping in and out of clouds now, and seeing was difficult. But certainly the blonde was recouping all the ground she might have lost. In the darkness of the night Eloise finally caught her breath, allowed herself to be covered by his dark jacket, and ran up the beach. Lucy, shaking her head in disgust, backed up to her own porch, and, when she bumped into the steps, sat down.

"Miss Borden? Lucy? Please don't go." Lucy's head snapped around. He *hadn't* gone up to the house with Eloise. He had turned and come back down the beach.

Lucy struggled to her feet. "We just came out to enjoy the moonlight," she muttered. "And that——"

"Crazy woman," he offered. "Did Maude——?"

"See them?" Lucy's hand was shaking. "I hope not. I sent her into the house, but—Lord knows what a child sees. And that's Eloise, the girl you plan to marry?"

"Damn!"

"That's probably—the appropriate word. Now perhaps you could gather up all the pieces and parts of your guests, so we——" she meant to say "decent," but was absorbed in the cultural shock against using judgmental words "—so we ordinary people can get some sleep."

"I'd like to come over later and explain," he murmured. Lucy jumped. She hadn't realized just how close he had come.

"I don't need any explanations," she hissed at him. "You can do as you please on your own property. Did you want to take Maude home with you?"

"No." He shoved both hands into his pockets in an act of disgust. "Why would I want to bring that sweet little kid back among——?"

"Why indeed?" Lucy asked in her most arctic tone. And a sprinkle of rain spattered off her nose. She blinked her eyes, and in that moment he was gone, lost in the gloom of the rising storm.

"So? Do I have to go back up there?" Maude asked. The child was waiting in the kitchen, holding on to the water taps as if she feared she might be swept away. And shivering. Lucy fumbled in the kitchen cupboard and found a jacket to slip over Maude's shoulders.

"No. Your father didn't want you to come back home. You'll still stay the night?"

"*That's* not my home. How could it be, with that crazy woman in it? I'd be happy to spend the night here. A lot of nights." The girl was wheezing, barely able to breathe. Oh, Lord, Lucy yelled at herself. The inhaler!

It was sitting on the edge of the kitchen cabinet, just where Lucy had placed it some hours before. Accustomed to all sorts of medical emergencies, as were most elementary schoolteachers, Lucy snatched off its plastic cover, pumped it in a test, then handed it over to Maude. The child sucked at its nipple, drawing in the rescuing gases. Gradually her shoulders ceased to shake as the spasm passed.

"So we'll have a cup of hot cocoa, and then we'll be off to bed," Lucy said as she wrapped one comforting arm around the thin shoulders. The girl coughed, found enough breath, and pressed closer to her.

"You too? It's only nine-thirty. Grown-ups don't go to bed that early."

Lucy's fingers were already busy assembling the drink, her mind a mile away. The child watched her face for a moment, and then slowly went up the stairs. What sort of a tangle is all this? Lucy was thinking. Her mother is dead. Her aunt plays naked on the beach. Her father thinks he can explain it all. Possible? It would have to be some almighty great explanation, no doubt about that. The milk she was stirring spat at her, managing to burn a little spot on her forefinger.

"There's nothing so much likely to bring you down to earth as a burnt finger," Lucy commented, and then looked around. "Maude?" There were noises from above. She carefully balanced a tray with the two mugs of cocoa, added a couple of biscuits for each, and made her way up the wide old staircase. "Maude?"

"In here." There were no lights on in the bedroom. Lucy stumbled across the open space, wound up purely by luck at the side of the bed, and managed to set the tray down on the bedside table. "Skill," she boasted as she flicked on the table lamp.

"Yeah," Maude replied. "I believe. No marshmallows?"

Lucy manufactured a shudder. "Not a chance. More calories to the ounce than chocolate whipped-cream cake. Drink."

"You know everything?" Maude was exploring cautiously.

"Not quite everything," Lucy admitted. "There are still one or two things I'm not quite sure of."

"Who fought the Battle of Jericho?" the child teased at her.

"See? What did I tell you? There's one of the things I don't know right there. Now, let's get this stuff down, and off to sleep."

"I don't get another riddle?"

"Rules of the game," Lucy said, and grinned down at her. The cup was quickly emptied, and balanced back on the tray. Lucastra picked it all up and made for the door. "Good night," she said. "And, oh—Joshua fought the Battle of Jericho!"

"You knew all the time," Maude complained.

Lucy turned and went downstairs, singing all she could remember of the old gospel hymn. "'Joshua fit the battle of Jericho, Jericho, Jericho, Joshua fit the battle of Jericho, and the walls came tumbling down!'"

"Show-off," Maude yelled from upstairs.

"Shut uppa you mouth, kid," Lucy yelled back, "or I gonna sing you in Italian!"

"No, no, don't do that," the girl squealed in gloriously faked terror. "Not that! Spare me!"

"Spare the rod and spoil the child," a very deep male voice said from just behind Lucy's left shoulder. It was too much. As Lucy whirled around the two mugs on the tray went sliding off and smashed into the corner of the stone fireplace.

"Oh——! You darn man! What the devil are you doing in my house?"

"What every father should do." He stepped out into the full light of the lamp. "Checking up on my child." The deep frown lines highlighted his face. Not a handsome man, no, not indeed. But a man who would stay the course? Lucy struggled with that idea for a moment or two. Was that the better trade-off? Bargain away tall, dark and handsome, in favor of big, tousled and dependable?

Lucy's budding anger was instantly pinched off. "Of course," she said softly. "Did you want to take a peek?"

"Not necessarily. If I do she'll be wide-awake again, and we'll be back to square one."

"It might be a good idea to go that far back," Lucy said. "After all, I missed all of square one, and don't even know what the devil square I'm in now. You know what, Mr. Proctor? You've got my curiosity bubbling like sixty. Why don't you sit down and let me get you a—drink? And then you can tell me about it."

He nodded and pulled out one of the kitchen chairs. "Old house," he commented casually.

Lucy's mind went off on another tangent, and she followed. "Old enough. Built by one of my ancestors in 1746."

"Ah. Land-proud Puritan?"

"No. House-proud Pilgrim. There was a large difference, you know."

"No, I don't know. I thought you were going to get me a drink."

"That I was," Lucy said, sighing in exasperation. "Only I don't have anything left in the bottle."

"You can't put me off with a grade-school excuse like that."

"I mean it," Lucy retorted. "The cupboard is bare. Unless——"

"Unless what?"

"Unless you've a great deal of nerve, Mr. Proctor."

"Jim," he said. "My name is James, but people call me Jim. What is it that requires so much nerve?"

"Peach brandy," she told him. "Homemade. My grandmother put it up just before she died."

"And how long ago was that?"

"Fifteen years ago, give or take a couple of months. Dare to try?"

He chuckled deep in his throat. Such a pleasant sound that Lucy's head snapped up. He *is* human, after all. Well, barely!

"If it hasn't broken the bottle by now it won't break my stomach," he pontificated.

"And that's what you think," Lucy muttered under her breath as she went for the bottle and the corkscrew. Things went from bad to worse in the pantry. She had no wine glasses; in fact, she had no water tumblers. The only thing available was her matched set of peanut-butter jars. So he'll know right away that we're not upper crust, she told herself as she measured him a massive dollop and marched out to set it in front of him.

He looked it over cautiously, then picked it up and sniffed. Lucy sat, tense. She knew the brandy had plenty of bouquet. He stared at the glass. "My mother had a matched set of glasses like this," he commented.

Yeah, I'll bet she didn't, Lucy thought. Look at the—monster—trying to get into my good graces by insinuating that his mother and I shared the same tastes in peanut-butter glasses. "How nice. Drink up."

He made a little toasting motion and slugged back the brandy. For a moment he maintained that teasing smile, and then suddenly his eyes rolled inward, his face turned a magnificent purple, and he began to choke.

Lucy jumped to her feet and began to pound on his back. He gasped for breath and waved her off. Water, she thought, and made a dash for the refrigerator, where the drinking water was stored in an old wide-mouthed milk bottle.

"Drink," she commanded as she poured the water where his mouth ought to be. And wasn't.

"Well, I'll say that for you," Lucy said some fifteen minutes later. "You've got a lot of nerve."

"I'm damn lucky you didn't drown me," he grumbled as he used her towel to dry himself off.

"Yes, there's that," she agreed anxiously. "Perhaps you'd like another glass of peach brandy?"

He had been standing in the middle of the kitchen, letting the water drip where it would. Now he came over to the table where she sat and tilted her chin up in his direction with a forefinger. "I don't need another thing in this house," he said. The words were spaced far apart, and each carried a load of sarcasm. "I wouldn't want you to do me any more favors. I wondered when I first met you why you were still unmarried, and now I know. You're a walking catastrophe!"

"What—what did you want to tell me about Maude?" she half whispered as she slipped out of her chair and backed away from him.

"Maude——" he roared, and then lowered his voice. "Maude has asthma," he said. "It doesn't bother her regularly, but, just in case, I had her bring her inhaler, and her medicine. I don't suppose that's too difficult for you to understand?"

"Not at all, Mr. Proctor," she said coolly. "Often I go for forty-eight hours or more without making a fool of myself. Was there anything else?"

That puzzled look was back on his face again. "I—no," he said. "But I did want to apologize for my—guests. I didn't think it would go that far. Eloise and I are staging a—reunion. I suggested she bring some of her friends down from Boston. But—it's only a one-time thing, you know."

"Apology accepted," she said. He could see by the stiffness of her shoulders, the firm line of her chin, that she meant no such a thing. And he could see by the soft curve of her breasts, the swelling of her hips, that he might do well to cultivate this girl. Maude liked her, and she wasn't as hard to look at as he had first thought. A girl worth knowing?

"What do you do—for a living?" he asked.

Surprised, Lucy turned from her job of mopping up the table and stared at him. He didn't seem to be setting a trap of any kind. "In the regular school year I am a permanent substitute in the local school system. During the summer I try my hand at anything that comes up."

"Anything?"

"Anything legal," she said, and then, catching the gleam in his eyes, "and moral! Hadn't you better get back to your guests?" And then added hesitantly, "Are you really going to get together with your sister-in-law?"

"Eloise," he said flatly. "Her name is Eloise. The walls *do* have ears in this neighborhood, don't they? Well, lest you die of curiosity, yes, she and I are seriously considering marriage, for Maude's sake, if not for anything else. And now, if I might go?"

"For Maude's sake?" What a stupid question, girl, she told herself as she nibbled on her lower lip. "For the Lord's sake!"

"For Maude's sake," he repeated. "Surely you can see that the girl needs a mother? A headstrong little thing, she is, and I don't have the time or the expertise to discipline her. I thought that Eloise, her mother's sister, would be just the ticket. And it would certainly make things a lot easier on her grandparents, who worship the ground Maude walks on."

"Ah—yes, I suppose so. Just the thing." Said very weakly. Lucy thought no such thing, but with the moonlight shining on him, reflecting his powers to command, she had no intention in the world to get on his bad side. From what she knew of him, he seemed to have a tremendously large bad side!

Lucy followed him out to the veranda, studying the firm wide shoulders that tapered down to narrow hips, the tremendous biceps that made him look nothing like a banker, the—pacing—like a jungle cat. I'd be doing him a favor if I stole him away from Eloise, she thought. I wonder if he's too much for *me*? I wonder how you go about stealing somebody's man away?

She took another look at the squared shoulders, marching as if on military parade. Just for the sake of it, she stuck her tongue out at him, only to see him stop and whirl and glower at her. She immediately swallowed her tongue, and offered him a gentle curtsy.

"That's more like it," he called, and headed back toward his own house.

"Yes, isn't it?" Lucy muttered to herself. I wonder if the library has a book on man stealing? But it wasn't libraries that held first place in her mind. At the earliest possible moment next day she went out and bought herself a new bathing suit, a beige one-piece that fitted in all the right places, but kept all the important parts covered.

CHAPTER THREE

THE house creaked and swayed as old houses did when Lucy Borden came back inside. The persistent drizzle had changed to a hard rain, drowning out both the sounds from the sea and the remaining noises from the next-door party. She went into the kitchen and put the kettle on.

Upstairs, the door to Maude's room was three-quarters closed. The light in the hall was enough to see by. Lucy peeped in, not wanting to disturb the child, and yet drawn to her. The bed was at the far side of the room, next to the window. Only a mass of blankets could be seen. That, and four sturdy fingers of one hand, which had escaped the confinement of the sheet. The child breathed deeply, with an almost musical note at the end of every exhalation. Just in case, Lucy checked the inhalator and the bottle of medicine, and stood them on top of the old bureau by the door.

Poor kid, she mused as she stole out of the room and walked down the stairs. He and his deceased wife's sister were going to try marriage because Maude needed a mother? Hardly the best of reasons for a wedding. Especially with a woman like Eloise. As Lucy already knew, the child thought of Eloise as the wicked stepmother, and that could only add problems to the joining. Asthma was sometimes a tension-driven disease.

The kettle whistled from downstairs. Lucy jumped, came back to present time, and went down to make herself a cup of tea. As it cooled she looked out of the back window, and down into the darkness, where the ocean made incessant play. In and out, in and out, seen or unseen, the mighty force that swayed continents tugged and splashed. "And forms all our futures," she told herself as she drank the tea.

Moments of indecision then, as she wandered around, out into the living room, by the tiny space that she called a library. Upstairs then, and into the bathtub, where hot water soothed her physical and mental woes. Of which there were many.

He's going to marry Eloise, she thought as she climbed out of the bath and grabbed a hot towel from the warming rack. Why would he do that when a much better substitute is standing right here? She turned to face the long mirror attached to the back of the door and made a face as her spirits plummeted.

Eloise was a tall, slim, long-limbed blue-eyed blonde. Her shoulder bones were barely covered with flesh. Her breasts, as best Lucy could remember from seeing by moonlight, were capacious—the kind that men in novels hungered for. And then there's you, Lucastra Borden.

Short, well-padded everywhere, firm, well-shaped breasts that stared back at her from the mirror with impudence. Brown hair, barely shoulder length because she hadn't the time to take care of anything longer. And green eyes. What could a brown-haired girl do with green eyes? No match. No match at all.

"So it's lucky I don't want him in the first place," she told herself haughtily as she toweled herself off, snatched up her nightgown, and headed for bed.

It might have been two o'clock in the morning when Lucy woke up with a start. A noise of some kind? Two of the wooden shutters on the upstairs windows facing the sea had a tendency to come loose. Shutters banging? Hardly.

Crying. A little girl, crying. And then footsteps pattering through the bathroom, and up to her door. "Can I come in? Please?"

Lucy sat up in bed and grabbed for her ancient green robe. "Of course you can." Her fingers found the switch on her night lamp, and a shadowy glow was cast over the room. Little Maude stood at the bathroom door, shifting her weight from foot to foot. Lucy beckoned, and the girl came across the room in a mad dash, throwing herself into Lucy's arms.

"What is it, love?"

"I—my bed."

"Your bed what?"

"It's wet. My bed's all wet."

Oh, wow, Lucy thought. Bed wetting? Anxiety syndrome. Tension. Of course! And the child needs sympathy. "Hey, now, accidents will happen. Come on, let's get you into a warm bath and I'll change your bed."

"It wasn't no accident."

"It wasn't? Here, let me get the water running, and let's get you out of this wet shirt."

"You believe me?"

"Why, of course I believe you. Who wouldn't?"

"*She* wouldn't." The young lips formed a straight line across the perturbed face. "She wouldn't believe nothin'."

"Ah. Put your fingers in. See if the water's not too hot."

"It's okay. What do I do with the shirt?"

"Just throw it in the corner there. I'll get it in a minute. How about these bath salts? Green bubbles?"

"I—that's swell. I don't get bath salts at home. You're not mad at me?"

"Of course I'm not. It could happen to anybody. Settle back now, and I'll turn on this little heater, and it'll make you all warm and comfortable. And I'll go check your bed."

"Be careful."

"Of course."

Be careful? Lucy teased herself with that as she bustled into the child's room and turned on the light. A quick one-handed pass over the bedsheets quickly convinced her that Maude was right. The bed was wet. The bed, to be honest, was soaked. Lucy was puzzled. She had no great experience with children's intimate needs, but there must be gallons of water on that bed.

She shook her head as she stripped off sheets all the way down to the mattress. And as she leaned over to finish the job a drop of cold water hit her right in the back of her neck.

"Oh, no," Lucy grumbled. She pulled back and looked up. Sure enough, the white calcimined ceiling sported a big dark circle. And forming in the middle of that dark circle was a massive drop of water—and then another—and then another!

"Maude," she called cheerfully. The splashing in the tub stopped. "Maude?" Lucy walked out into the bathroom. "Not to worry. You're not at all responsible for the wet bed."

"Well, of course I'm not," the girl responded. "Did you——? You did, didn't you? You thought I wet the bed!" The child's eyes were solemn round circles in her dark skin. "There's a hole in your roof!" Added indignantly, as if it were a major crime to have a hole in the roof.

"So there, you see?" Lucy knelt down beside the bathtub and accepted a wet hug from a dripping head of curls. "And that's why I'm nobody's mother. I don't have the—intuition."

"Don't worry," the little girl told her. "You could learn. But first you've got to fix the roof."

"But first I've got to know somebody in some bank who'd be willing to loan me some money," Lucy said, shaking her head. "A very hard job, borrowing money from a bank. They'd rather not lend money unless they're sure you don't need it."

"I know lots of people in a bank," Maude said. "Why don't you and I go visit one of them tomorrow?"

"That *would* be a nice idea," Lucy said, but her heart was not in the words, and even the child could hear the skepticism. She had already toured most of the banks in the area, to no avail. But still, if the sun came out in the morning it might be well worth the try. Early in the morning, because *that man* would want his daughter back pretty quickly!

"Come on, love. You'll have to share my bed for the rest of the night."

Lucy tossed and turned that night. Not accustomed to sharing a bed, she told herself sleepily as she stared over at the tiny sprawled figure beside her. "I wonder what time banks open for business?"

"Nine o'clock," Maude replied. "Go to sleep, Lucy. Everything will be all right."

Yes, I'm sure it will, Lucy told herself as she tucked both her hands under her pillow and thus under her neck. Loans for repairs. Why not build a new house? It would be wide and spacious, but with low ceilings, so that any tall dark-haired man would have to bend over or break his head. And, given enough training, such a man would become subservient, and he would bow down in front of Little Lucy and do everything she commanded—and a few things for which Lucy did not yet know the commands.

So when she woke up, stiff and perspiring, Lucastra Borden was...happy...to escape from her erotic dreams.

"My dad's bank is up here," Maude directed. "At the corner of the Highway and Main Street." Lucy knew it for sure. Not more than a year ago it had been her last stop in the grand tour, trying unsuccessfully to get a loan. But there were a few new faces to be seen in the loans department. Maude, with all the brashness of childhood, led her directly to the desk of "John Ledderman, Loan Officer." A very impressive sign, brass on mahogany. And a very impressive young man. Well, perhaps not that young. He fitted all the descriptions. Tall, dark, handsome—and the owner of the "approval" pen that might turn the Borden domicile into a thing of pride and perfection. Lucy tried him out with a Class II smile. Maude pushed her way in front and said, "Mr. Ledderman. You remember me? Maude Proctor. My daddy owns this bank."

Which, Lucy thought, was about as complete an introduction as a loan officer might need. "Of course," he said. The voice was a disappointment. It should have been a nice baritone. Instead it played in the upper tenor range, and occasionally squeaked. "Of course—er—Maude. What can I do for you?"

"This is my friend Lucastra Borden—Lucy," the girl said, bowing out of the way.

"Lucy Borden?" Mr. Ledderman was obviously scavenging in his memory. And his eyes lit up.

"Lucastra Borden! Well, what a pleasure it is to meet you!"

"It is?" She brushed her long brown hair back off her face. The man obviously had mistaken her for some other Lucy Borden.

"Of course it is, Miss Borden. Or may I call you Lucy?"

She waved a hand vaguely. He could call her all the names in the Bible if only he was prepared to grant a loan.

"Lucy Borden," he said. "Imagine that. My fiancée and I were just talking about you last night."

And now I'm beginning to feel like the third-row comedian in the burlesque, Lucy thought. And only one thing to say. "Oh, were you?"

"Yes, indeedy." His eyes gleamed. His teeth sparkled at her. He was rubbing both hands together as if he had the ten-year itch. "Yes, indeedy," he repeated. "Mary Norris. Nurse Norris, over at the Merit Nursing Home. She told me—well, that's not important. How may I help you—er—Lucy?"

"I need to——" Lucy started out, but the words would not quite form in her mouth. She coughed, took a deep breath, and started out at full speed. "I need to borrow ten thousand dollars to fix up my house." Period; time to breathe again. He was still smiling, so she hadn't thrown him off his feed at all. He gestured her to a chair.

"Is that all?"

"I—yes, that's all—for the moment."

"Sometimes it's better to borrow more than you need," he suggested gently.

"But my house isn't very——"

"Not to worry." He actually laughed, and people at all the other desks turned to look. He shrugged his shoulders and readjusted his coat, and then in softer tones, "Banks often make loans on intangibles, Lucy. And you have great expectations. You and Mrs. Moore, of course."

"Well, then," Lucy announced, "why don't we make that twenty thousand? Just in case, of course! Where do I sign?"

"Oh, it takes a little more than that," he said, sighing. She could see it hurt him not to be able to reach into the bottom drawer and pull out the money. "About a day, I would suspect. And I'll bring the papers to you, if that's agreeable."

"Oh, that's—yes," Lucy said excitedly. "Where were you last year when I needed you?"

"I—er—beg pardon?"

"Nothing. Nothing. Yes, that's fine. That's excellent. I'll be at home all day tomorrow. You'll bring the money?"

"Not exactly," he said with a chuckle hiding behind the words. "The money will be deposited in an account in your name here at the bank. I'll bring you a check book you can use."

"Well, it's certainly a pleasure doing business with you," she stammered. "I would hate to have to do business with Mr. Proctor. That man gives me—well, he does.''

"Isn't that strange how different people have different reactions?" he said. "We all find Mr. Proctor to be a fine man. And of course there's the Scout troop which we now sponsor, and I believe he's on the board at the Congregational Church, and the Little League team——"

"Must be some other Proctor," Lucy muttered. "Come on, Maude."

At the front door the child tugged her to a stop. "Hurry up," Lucy muttered. "He might change his mind!"

The pair of them stole out of the glass double doors, only to find that the fox behind them was only half as scary as the wolf before. There, poised on the top one of the four cement steps, was Jim Proctor.

"Well. No wonder I could find neither hair nor hide of you," the gruff low voice said. "Well?"

"G'morning, Daddy. Lucy wanted to see what your bank looked like."

"A likely story," he rumbled. He was banker dressed. A dark single-breasted suit, off-white shirt and dull blue tie. Altogether boring, Lucy decided, but she did an unusual thing for her. She held her tongue.

"I wanted you to spend the day with Eloise," Proctor told his daughter. "We have a great deal of adjusting to do, and not much time."

"But Daddy, last night we——"

"No excuses." Genghis Khan must have sounded like that on one of his better mornings, Lucy thought. Take the rascal out, give her a fair trial, and then—the executioner!

"I want you to go home now," he continued. "Eloise is waiting for you. And I'll be along shortly to see that things are going well! Is there something you wanted to say, Miss Borden, or are you just choking to death?"

"I have a great deal I want to say," Lucy said firmly. She cleared her throat.

"But not here and now," Proctor interrupted. "Maude, climb in my car. Frank will drive you back home."

"But Lucy will——"

"It's a lovely day," he said, and now there was a grim expression on his face. It might possibly be classified as a smile, but not very. "I'm sure Miss Borden would be happy to have time for a walk in the sunshine."

And there, right before her eyes, the girl was popped into the Cadillac, the banker nodded to Lucy in passing, and she was all alone on the steps. But the doors opened again and the bank president stuck his head out. "I'm glad you've seen my bank," he said. "I hope you won't come again. I shudder to think of what might happen if we had to transact business, you and I." And this time he was gone for good.

"Yeah," Lucy muttered under her breath. "I should live so long." And, since the nursing home was only down the street, she wandered in that direction.

This was to be a day of unusual activities, no doubt about it. As Lucy rounded the corner she noted considerable toing and froing in front of the nursing home. A big moving van was parked directly in front of the door, and two or three other cars crowded in on either side. Men were carrying furniture *out* of the building.

Inside, a cluster of nurses and aides were gathered around the nursing station. The din of the chatter overrode every other noise. Lucy, not being able to get a word in edgewise, shrugged her shoulders and went on to Angie's room, to find further confusion.

"What in heaven's name are you doing in that wheelchair, Angie?"

"Oh, Lucy! Thank the Lord you've come!" There were tears in the faded blue eyes. One of the old lady's hands was nervously plucking at the fringe of the blanket that covered her legs.

"Yes," Lucy said. "Why?"

"You hadn't heard? I thought that's why you came!"

"No. I haven't heard. What haven't I heard?"

Full tears now, running down the time-ravaged cheek, dripping off the corners of a trembling mouth. "The bank. They've foreclosed on the mortgage of the home. We all have to be out of here within twenty-four hours! I don't know where to go!"

Foreclosed! No wonder he looked so cheerful, Lucy mused. Jim Proctor at his best. Let's beat up on some poor beggar, and foreclose on the elderly ill, all before breakfast! Not for a moment did she consider that there were three other banks in town, any one of which might have done the deed. As far as Lucastra Borden was concerned, this was a move programmed and planned only by the arch villain of them all, James Proctor.

Practical little Lucastra shifted gears. She managed a smile as she offered Angie a tissue. "What do you mean, you don't know where to go, love? You'll come to me, that's what you'll do. All those empty rooms I have, and you worry about where to go?"

"But Lucy, you can't spare all that much time to take care of me. That's a terrible job."

"Not so terrible. Besides, I haven't found a smell of a summer job. We have until school opens in September before anything becomes a real problem. Now, I'll walk home to get the car, and you have the nurses pack you up and all that stuff. Okay?"

The tears were wiped out in an instant. "I've always wanted to live by the beach again," Angie confided. "These people are nice, but—you'll be right back?"

"Right back. Promise." Lucy leaned over and kissed the furrowed brow. "And, besides, think of how much better the food will be!"

* * *

Lucy's car was a real antique. Purchased by her grandfather prior to World War II, the eight-cylinder black Packard had been up on blocks for so many years that it had been forgotten. Until the local garage mechanic had decided to pay off his debts to Lucastra by putting it back on the road. Now, laden with all the odds and ends that Angie Moore possessed, it was parked out in front of the house as Lucy tried to manhandle Angie's belongings inside.

It was hard going, especially when the afternoon sun took command of the skies. So when the big car pulled up behind her and a cheery voice said, "Need some help?" she sighed with relief.

"Do I ever?" she said as she turned around to look. "All the help I can get. I'd even recruit Lucifer if he—Oh! You!"

"As you said, even Lucifer." He was laughing as he climbed out of the driver's seat of the Cadillac. There was something different about him. More than the way he was dressed, although that was startling. Blue jeans and a white boat-necked sweater. A pair of well-worn espadrilles, but no socks. No, it was something else. Perhaps the wide smile? Or the look in his eyes? And why not? she reminded herself. He's had all morning to do his foreclosures.

"Made your quota for the day?" she asked.

"Quota?"

"Don't tell me your bank doesn't have a quota on foreclosures!"

He cocked his head to one side, and studied her face and figure, line by line. "Quotas," he mused. "Don't tell me. It'll come to me sooner or later."

But in the meantime, Lucy told herself, I need the labor. Look at those muscles! I wonder if he pumps iron—or maybe he gets his exercise picking up girls to throw onto his bed? Her face turned red as she turned away from him.

"All this stuff in the car," she gestured. "We're making Angie a bedroom out of my downstairs library. That's where it goes."

"Make some coffee," he ordered as he seized almost half the load in the car's back seat, and then did a double take. "A 1934 Packard," he said reverently, running his free hand down across the glittering black finish. "Does it run?"

"Of course it runs," Lucy snapped.

"Okay, okay, I was just asking. I knew all you collectors were jealous, but——"

"Lift that barr'l," she ordered. *Collectors*? He lifted and bustled, and the screen door slammed behind him. Angie Moore was sitting in her wheelchair in the middle of the living room. Always interested, the old lady's eyes lit up.

"Well, I do declare," she declared. "Little Jimmy Proctor!"

"Ma'am?"

"You don't remember me?"

"I—guess not, ma'am."

"And stop *ma'aming* me. I used to whomp your bottom three or four times a year for stealing apples off my tree. Family lived two doors down in those days. You were a *little* rascal then. Now look at you. How you have changed!"

His grin was infectious. She grinned back. "Yes, ma'am," he said. "Changed a great deal since. I've become much taller."

"But still the rascal?"

"Well——" He debated. "Hard to admit it, being a banker and all."

"Don't tell me," Angie chuckled. "Tall and handsome, and employed to boot?"

"As you say." Gradually it was all coming back to him. The little old lady, much younger then. Spritely, full of charm. Whacked you for stealing her apples, and then offered lunch while you recuperated. And it was better to be whacked by Angela Moore than be reported to his father, whose hand left a much more prominent reminder!

Angie's grin disappeared. "Might need you about, Jim Proctor," she said very softly. "Got me a problem. You're not married, are you?"

"Not—at the moment," he admitted.

"Good. There's a wonderful girl outside there. Wonderful. Lacks only one thing. She needs to be married. That's her forte in life."

His smile faded as well. The *wonderful* girl outside, the threat to life and limb? The neighborhood wrecker? She needs to be married? Draw me a diagram, Mrs. Moore!

"Who says?" he said.

"Me. I said. Girl needs a husband to fulfill her. A husband and two or three children. That's her purpose in life. Good doing. And she's especially good with children. You'd make a fine pair, you and Lucy."

"Hey, well, just wait a minute." He set part of his load down on the floor. "Out of training," he commented as he rubbed his arm muscle. "You think I would plunge into marriage just to fulfill that woman? I've been down the marriage route. In fact, I've a young daughter of my own to look out for."

"Do you say so?" Angie crowed. "Just the thing. No one in town is better at mothering than Lucy Borden."

"So why hasn't she been mothering her own for years past? She's not exactly a spring chicken." And yes, he thought, Lucy and Maude—I've never seen a better matched pair. But hell, I can't keep shifting gears. I've got Eloise primed to move in. One's enough. But—there was that magic word. Tall, skinny Eloise. She might make a wonderful mother, but racked up in bed she was all bone ends and bad temper. A man could get splinters trying to hug that woman. On the other hand, Lucy Borden looked to be as delightful a handful as any man could—— Come on now, Proctor. You're too far down the road to shift now!

He picked up his load again. Walk softly, he warned himself. "And where does all this go?" Angie was nodding her wise old head as she pointed out the directions. She would answer his question later.

There were voices disputing as he went back out to the car. Arguing? Well, only one was doing that. A shrill soprano voice beating against a serene baritone. "Eloise? What are you doing down here?"

"Among other things," his fiancée yelled at him, and then stopped for a deep breath—and a shot of wisdom, Lucy told herself as she loaded her arms with more goods. "I—think it must be the heat," Eloise said. "Something's affecting my temper. But no matter, as long as I've found you. You promised to take me sailing, love, and you're already an hour late." The tall blonde came over beside him, and her voice level dropped. "And to find you playing with the neighborhood—er—witch, James?" A little laugh, as if they were sharing a secret.

"Careful, Eloise." His big hand squeezed her shoulder tightly enough to draw a wince. "We don't use that sort of language outside the big cities." She winced under his hand—almost brought to tears by the pressure. "Miss Borden here is our neighbor."

"Of course she is." Eloise broke out into a scale-climbing giggle. "And don't think—Lucinda, is it? Don't think that I'm not grateful to you, looking after Maude. It's hard for a person my age to get along with children. Oh, I'll learn, of course, but it takes time. Now Jim and I—we're almost of an age, which explains why he gets along with me better than he does with you."

"Thank you," Lucy offered. "I didn't think I was all that much younger than you—but thank you anyway."

"Oh, my. How moralizing we are." The blonde stepped back a pace, and changed the subject. "We're still not too late for a sail, Jim."

He checked his wristwatch. "No, of course we aren't. Where's Maude?"

"Surely you don't——? Yes, where is the little darling? We'll have such a good time, you with all your navy skills, darling!"

"Surely I do," he said grimly. "That's the whole purpose of the exercise. But you have to learn, Eloise. Two years on a nuclear submarine did nothing at all to qualify me to sail a sloop. Now, where is the child?"

"I haven't the slightest idea," Eloise said. "Not the slightest. She refused to eat her lunch, and then buzzed off somewhere."

"Lucy," he leaned in her direction, "I'll send a couple of men down from the house. Keep them for the rest of the day if you need them. They're great for lifting and hauling." And then, as a sort of afterthought, "Is Mrs. Moore going to spend some time in your house? I knew her when I was—considerably younger."

"Yes. Angie's going to stay with me." Her normally cheerful voice had become strained, arctic. "She was living in the Merit Nursing Home, you know."

He nodded, latched on to Eloise's thin arm, and started off up the beach at high speed. Well, of course he knows, Lucy told herself as she folded her arms across her breasts and watched the pair of them. You can hardly foreclose on a big business like that without giving some thought to the welfare of the patients. Or could you? Dr. Jekyll? Mr. Hyde? He seemed so—pleasant—today.

The men arrived in less than ten minutes, both Cape natives, happy to deviate from their normal day's work. By noontime Angie's new room was organized.

"Not everything's finished," Lucy said as she opened the door of the cupboard in the new room. Ordinarily it would have been full of spare books, waiting to be stored or sold. And now it was filled with...

"Yes, I can see there's work to do," Angie commented as she wheeled closer to the door. Lucy, who had been looking at Angie all this time, caught the devilish look in the old lady's eyes and turned to look in the cupboard.

"Maude Proctor!"

"So that's the little Proctor girl," Angie said. "Land's sakes!"

"What are you doing in there?" Lucy had to struggle for her voice-of-doom sound. The girl was huddled against the back wall, a determined look on her face, and saying not a word.

"Hiding is what she's doing," Angie said. "Little girls do a lot of that. Or at least they did in my time. The questions arise—why, and from whom?"

Maude made not a sound. Her eyes followed Lucy for a moment, and then switched back to Angie. "Well, you needn't stare at me like that," the old woman said. "If I had been up to speed some years ago I could have been your grandmother." Angie turned to Lucy to explain. "Alfred was a wonderful man and I was—well, back in the twenties I was known as a flapper. Would you believe that?"

Lucy, who was willing to believe almost anything about anybody, looked puzzled. "But——"

"I wasn't fast enough," Angie interrupted. "There was another candidate in the running. His mother's candidate, so to speak."

"But——"

"Don't stutter, Lucy. There's a dear girl. No, I was a little too naive at the time. My—opponent—claimed she was pregnant. And in those days, my dear, there was only one possible solution. Alfred married her."

"Dear me."

"Yes. Their first child was not born until fourteen months later. They just made it, even using the Napoleonic code. And I, of course, was heartbroken. Well, for a month or more I pined, and then I took a cruise to the Caribbean, and I met—well, that's another story."

Maude stirred. "And you really, truly were almost my grandmother?"

"Really, truly, child. Come out of there. Nobody keeps closets entirely clean these days."

"Yes," Lucy commanded. "Come out of there." And how did I suddenly become the second banana in my own house? she asked herself, bemused. "And just what are you hiding from?"

"Liver," Maude declared. "Liver and broccoli. She was going to make me eat it for lunch. Yuck!"

"Well, I ought to send you straight home," Lucy retorted. "Your father is angry enough with me already, without having all this runaway business!"

"I wasn't running away from my father," Maude declared. "He's nice. Just from the liver. And her." And then a little grin. "Besides, it's too late. I just saw the sloop leave the dock."

"Lucastra? Didn't you say you had some business to transact? Why don't you leave the child with me? She can help me unpack."

Yes, why don't I? Lucy asked herself. Why do I feel as if the world has turned upside down? Why am I taking orders in my own home, and mooning around after that—man next door, as if he were some prize in the lottery?

But, being an eminently practical person, she shook herself out of her daydreams and went on down to the kitchen and the telephone. As she consulted the yellow pages for builders she could hear the ripples of laughter coming to her from the bedroom. Young laughter—old laughter. That's your problem, Maude, Lucy thought as she dialed the appropriate number. Angie should really have been your grandmother!

CHAPTER FOUR

THE builder arrived the next afternoon, hardly an hour after the bank's loan officer, John Ledderman, had come by with a new bank passbook, and a check book to match. All three of them gathered around the wide table that the builder had set up in the sand behind the house. Some of his drawings were already rolled out in the sun. Ledderman wore coat and tie, the banker's uniform. Henderson was dressed in a T-shirt and a pair of blue jeans that might well have seen the D-Day battle in France. Lucy was somewhat pleased with herself. Her lovely pink sundress was cool, comfortable, and blew around her knees in the consistent onshore wind.

"Terrible, wasn't it," the bank officer commented, "closing down the Merit Home and all? My fiancée was all broken up about it, but she's been offered a job down at Toby Hospital. You know, I always say that whatever happens is always for the best?"

"Do you always say that?" Lucy muttered. "Is this where I sign?"

"Right there, where the X mark is," he instructed. "Yes, that's what I always say."

"Ain't what I always say," Mr. Henderson, the builder, commented. "Damn bankers. Ruined the country in 1932, they did, and doin' their best to do it again."

"Oh, I don't know," the bank's man said. "Can't blame greed just on the bankers. There's enough blame to be scattered all around. Well, best of luck, Miss Lucastra. I'm sure you'll have enough money on hand for——"

"Needs a new roof," Henderson interrupted, glaring at the banker.

"Best of luck to you and your fiancée," Lucy said hastily. Out of the corner of her eye she had seen That Man stalking down the beach in their direction, two of his hired men behind him, and she wanted to avoid any further confrontations. She took Ledderman's arm and hustled him around the corner of the house to his car. By the time she got back to her builder he and That Man were having a conversation. Jim Proctor seemed to know a great deal about building—or perhaps it was the other way around? Perhaps she had chosen a builder who couldn't tie his shoes in the dark?

"No," Henderson was saying, "it ain't exactly that the joists is bendin'. Been up there for many a year, they has. The problem is that the foundation's sinkin' on the east side there. Happening to most every house on the Cape, you know. Place is only a sand pile that's being blown or washed away. I suspect, Mr. Proctor, that your house will fall over before this one does. All the new places, they're built just on the sand." He stopped and stared at the banker as he wiped the back of his neck with an old red kerchief. Proctor maintained a stone face. The builder gave a dry coughing chuckle.

"Like in the Good Book," he chortled. "Them as build on sand, or something." Proctor offered a tiny smile. "All the old houses, like Miss Lucastra's here, they're built on whatever rock could be found. And don't, for goodness' sake, buy a house across the canal. That land over there is erodin' faster than your dog can spit!"

"Well, that's a relief," Proctor answered. "I don't have a dog. Just a little lost daughter." He turned around and looked speculatively at Lucy. Behind him his two guards were studying the ground like a pair of hound dogs.

Footprints in the sand, Lucy asked herself. After they tramp over everything? "Gone again?" She folded her hands behind her back, crossing a pair of fingers on each one. And tried her best to look innocent.

"Gone again," he agreed. "You wouldn't——?"

"Me? No, I wouldn't——"

"I thought not," he replied. "But you'll run her back up to the house if you should see her?"

"Of course. That's what neighbors are for. Somebody will be there all day?"

"Yeah." He didn't sound as if he believed a word of what she had to say. He put both hands in his pockets and rocked back and forth on his heels for a moment, all the while examining Lucy from head to toe. The slight onshore breeze tussled with his hair, ruining his dignity. It didn't seem to bother him particularly, but he did try to comb it down with his fingers.

"I'm glad to see you've decided to improve your property," he said. "It'll do all of us in the neighborhood some good. You managed to get a bank loan?"

Lucy scuffed her bare toe in the sand and looked away from him. "Yes. A loan."

He shook his head slowly from side to side. "You were lucky," he said. "I don't know what the banking business is coming to. One of these days the whole shebang is going to collapse."

"My house?"

"My business," he said, chuckling. "What sensible banker would loan you money on this——?"

"Well, I have—hidden assets," she assured him.

"You surely do." Her head snapped up just in time to discover that his roving eye had stopped just about at the level of her breasts, where the wind was pressuring her thin cotton bodice tightly against them.

"I didn't mean anything like that," she snapped. "Don't be a voyeur! Can't a girl have some peace of mind even in her own backyard?"

"No. I mean—yes." There was a puzzled tone in his voice, as if he had lost his train of thought completely. "Yes. Of course. Some bright young loan officer is going to make a bundle off this project. Or lose his shirt." And then, in a more friendly tone, "Glad to run into you again, Henderson. Give the lady a good show for her money." He offered Lucy a one-fingered salute, and sauntered off back up the beach.

"For *your* money," Lucy whispered under her breath. Her fingers gradually unfolded. She could not repress the sigh of relief that escaped her.

"Good man, that," Henderson said. "Now, about that roof?"

"Yeah, about that roof." Lucy was following the slow progress of the two guards back up the beach in the wake of their boss. Good man? Zooming up the beach like a cruise ship being chased by a couple of Boston whalers? Good for what? Pictures formed in her mind. A dark rainy night, with a fire going in her bedroom. Everything right and tight, Bristol fashion, and he—what is he doing, lying on my bed with no shirt on?

"Miss Lucy?"

"Oh. Yes. The roof," she said, sighing. All that lovely money, she thought, sitting safely in his bank. More money than she had seen in a dollop of years. Homing-pigeon money? Here today and gone tomorrow? "Yes, fix the roof, Mr. Henderson. And somehow we need another bathroom downstairs."

"Cost a mint of money," he drawled.

"Fix it all. Fix everything." Her voice went up half an octave, as if she was on the edge of hysteria. "I've finally come into money, Mr. Henderson. Somebody else's money. And when he finds out he'll—oh, Lord, my ship has come in!''

"Ayup," Henderson said as she turned on her heel and headed around the side of the house. The Henderson family had its share of strange members, too. So maybe her ship *had* come in. Loaded with all the profits of the Orient, of course, just as the old New England expression meant it to be. "Fix everything. Why not? Always knew them Bordens had it stacked away someplace." He scratched the bald spot on the top of his head. "Come on," he bellowed to his crew, "let's get to work!"

Angie Moore was humming away as she moved her wheelchair over into the bright light coming in through the south window. She stopped and smiled when Lucy came in. "They don't design houses to fit the world any more," she commented. "In the old days you'd never find a house that didn't have windows on the south wall, for the winter sunshine."

"You're right," Lucy agreed. "I don't suppose you would have seen little Maude around any place, would you? No—don't tell me. I really don't want to know. I——"

"Seems to me you spend more time worrying about *him* than anything else you do," the old lady said. "And that telephone's been ringing like a dog with burrs in his bottom."

"What him?" Lucy snapped.

"That him. The one who lives next door. Lost his daughter again, has he?"

"Yes, and we're immediately suspects. Coming down here like a sheriff's posse, trailing those two gun goons behind him. Eight people he has working in that house, would you believe it? Besides himself, of course. You'd think that eight people would be able to keep track of one little girl, wouldn't you?"

"Yes—well—she claimed she had to go to the bathroom, and couldn't wait to go back up to the other house. I couldn't tell her to go home, could I?"

"Don't tell me," Lucy pleaded. "I don't want to know. I really don't want to know. What telephone calls?"

"Answers to your advertisement in the newspaper. The one about girls for a swimming club here along the beach. I wrote their names and phone numbers down. They're on the desk under the telephone. Say, I'm glad the bank foreclosed on that nursing home. I haven't been so busy, or had so much fun, in a dog's age! Got my blood up, it has."

"Yeah, well, we'd better take care not to cross That Man." Strange how the capital letters could be plainly heard in her voice. "I don't care to get mixed up with him, and if his daughter is—no, I don't want to know."

Angela Moore chuckled. "You don't care to get mixed with him? Lucy Borden, telling lies like that!"

"I'm not lying," she said desperately. "I'm not. He's—I'm——"

"Yes, that's about the whole of it, Lucy. Don't fight it. Love is a very fine thing, and he's a fine young man, Jimbo is. And it's printed all over your lovely little face that you're for him."

Lucy felt the trap closing in all around her. She grabbed for the arms of the morris chair and settled into it. The old springs squeaked comfortably. She managed a couple of deep breaths. "Jimbo?"

"Jimbo. That's what the whole neighborhood called him when he was five years old. You don't hear that kind of thing around these parts any more."

"I am not in love with the man," Lucy said, speaking slowly and distinctly, the way one spoke to idiots and small children.

"So you say."

"I'm not!" She struggled to the edge of the big chair, her eyes alight with anger. "I suppose you've been in love, and have lots of experience?"

Mrs. Moore giggled as she rolled her chair over beside Lucy. "Me? Of course I've been in love. Lots of times! But in my day one didn't go about boasting about *experience*, my dear. The word had different connotations when I was young. So what are you doing to do—run from him, or after him?"

"I'm going to—hide." Lucy set her stubborn jaw and bounced out of the chair. "I'm going to be the mistress of a fine swimming club." She moved purposefully over to the desk and the list of prospective students.

"Yes, run and hide," Angie called after her. "Women did that all the time in my day, to their regret. You'd find it more fun to be *his* mistress, love."

Lucy struggled upstairs to the bathroom. The palms of her hands were hurting. Not until she stood in front of the mirror did she note her fists were clenched, her own nails biting into her skin hard enough to leave marks. "Damn that man!" The words burst out without her volition. The drapes of the shower curtain rattled. Little Maude stuck her head out.

"My dad, you mean? Has he gone?"

"Maude Proctor!"

The shower curtain rattled closed. Well, Lucy Borden, she told herself, you've been bringing it all down on yourself. If you hadn't been so *motherly* earlier you wouldn't be in this position. You should have been hard-nosed with the child. *Motherly*! What a terrible word that was! But there was no use frightening the child.

Gently she pulled the curtains open. The girl was huddled in a corner, crouched down, shivering. "There's no need for that, Maude. Nobody's going to eat you."

"Hah! What do *you* know?"

"Maude." Lucy was feeling put upon. "Come on, child, get out of my shower this instant!"

The girl stirred, sliding along the side of the tub, keeping out of reach. As she stood up she said, "I'm not going back there. Not ever."

Lucy loaned her a hand as she stepped out. "Strong words," she said softly. "Then where *are* you going?"

"I was gonna stay here, but now I can see you're a mean grown-up too, just like him. I don't know what I'm going to do, but I'm not going back there." The child managed to get free of the tub and shower curtain, and then backed stiffly away. Bells rang in Lucy's mind. Four years of teaching had left her with some definite opinions of children's reactions.

"Maude? What's the matter?"

"Nothin's the matter." The girl seemed to huddle in on herself, wrapping her arms around her stomach and moving to be sure that her back was not exposed to Lucy's eyes.

"Just like him?"

"I tried to tell him, but he wouldn't listen." The girl moved further away. Strange, Lucy thought, she's wearing a light cotton blouse, and it seems to be sticking to her in places. And there's that smell.

"Tell me what you were going to tell him," she said gently.

"Why? You couldn't do nothin' about it. He don't even—like you." At which the child bent over in agony and the tears began to run. Lucy tried to touch her, but Maude was having none of that. She moved again, evading Lucy's grasp. The tears bubbled on. "That was a lie," the girl sobbed. "He *does* like you a lots."

"Maude, take off your blouse."

"No!"

"Maude, take off that blouse or I'm going to take it off for you."

"You wouldn't dare—would you?"

"You'll find out in a minute, girl."

"All right, all right, I—— It's stuck." The child struggled with the front buttons on the little white blouse until Lucy moved in and undid the buttons for her. The little stick arms slid out of the short sleeves with some trouble. Lucy turned her around gently, and managed to pull the blouse free from Maude's back, where it had been glued by traces of some liquid. That smell again. What was it? Working gently, Lucy stripped the blouse off the bare back.

"My Lord in heaven," Lucy snapped. "Who did this?"

The child's back was wet by a thick viscous liquid. Lucy sniffed. It had been a long time since her grandfather had tilted his bottle regularly. His favorite drink, brandy. And the child's back and blouse were soaked with it.

"Who did this? Did your father——?"

"My dad wouldn't do a thing like that," the child defended fiercely.

"Then who?" The little chin went up. Lucy knew there would be no answer—but was one needed? Slowly she could feel the Borden anger rise. If he didn't do it, he knew who was responsible for doing it! Without further thought she draped a soft bath towel around the girl's shoulders and snatched up one of her hands. "Come on!"

They rattled down the stairs, the girl putting up a minimum resistance. "Oh, my!" Mrs. Moore exclaimed as they went by her at flank speed. "What's that awful bar-room smell?"

Lucy, who was carrying the child's blouse in her other hand, grimaced. "You can say that again," she snarled. The screen door banged behind them as they went down onto the sand.

"Somethin' wrong?" Mr. Henderson stopped his work for a moment.

"Not now," Lucy snarled. "But very soon!"

"Need any help, you just call me."

Lucy stared at the double muscles on his arms. He looked as if he might demolish a tank with a single blow. But not yet. "Maybe later," she called as they zoomed by him.

"I don't wanna go in that house," Maude said as they passed the rock that was the boundary between the two houses. Moving her became a tug-of-war.

"You might as well give up," Lucy said. "I'm stronger than you are. Do you want him to see you dragged along as if you were Ruprecht?"

"He'll be mad," Maude cried. "He'll be awful mad. I don't want to see him mad like that. I don't wanna——!"

"He deserves it," Lucy almost shouted, and then managed to get herself under control again. "He deserves every little bit of it! Come on, now, Maude, stop the crying. You're going to get even.''

"I am?'' The child's face lightened as she hurried to catch up. "I didn't 'zactly see it like that.''

"You ought to,'' Lucy said as they climbed up onto the back porch of the Proctor home. "Women don't have to put up with this sort of thing any more. Not in these days and times.''

One of the guards was standing at the glass sliding door that led into the house. "Hey, you found her,'' he said. "The boss will be glad to——''

"The boss might not be all that happy,'' Lucy interrupted grimly. "Open the door.'' The man barely managed to slide the door away before Lucy's foot reached it. Inside, everything was quiet, almost as if they had entered a sanctuary.

"Where the devil is somebody?'' Lucy yelled. Her words echoed down the hall and bounced around the far end of it. "Somebody?'' came echoing back to her. "Where the devil is somebody?'' she yelled again. There was a crashing sound as one of the far doors opened and slammed shut.

"What's going on?'' He had a pencil cocked behind his ear, and a sheaf of papers in his right hand. "Ah . . . Miss Proctor, I believe?''

The child moved behind Lucy's back, still shuddering.

"What can I do for you, Lucy?''

"The first thing you can do is call the police. The second thing you can do is stop trying to be a funny guy. The third thing you can do is remember that my name is Miss Borden!''

"Well, you do have a want list, don't you?"

"Just call the police, you—you monster!"

The pleasant expression faded from his face. He beckoned to the guard, and sent him off into the next room, where a telephone was hidden. "Perhaps you'd better tell me about it," he said. His voice was soft but commanding. Threatening too. Lucy shivered to match Maude. He was a very big man; a very threatening man.

"Maybe *I'd* better call the police," she muttered as she backed away from him.

"Maybe you'd better sit down in that chair." He pointed toward one of the Hepplewhite chairs standing in a grim line against the wall. Lucy sidled in that direction, finally easing herself into one of the chairs. Its cold bottom did the same to her own, even though she had carefully gathered her skirts up beneath her. Maude walked stiffly over next to the same chair, but remained standing, leaning against the wall. He glared at them for an additional moment.

"Now just what the devil's wrong?" he asked, his voice kept level at a modified roar. "I come home to find the entire house in an uproar."

"Throwing alcohol at children is called child abuse," Lucy said bravely. "It's a terrible crime. Maybe if you——"

"What the hell are you talking about?" He was up out of his chair, and took a step or two forward.

"You can't intimidate me," Lucy told him, but didn't believe a thing she was saying. He can intimidate me very easily, she thought anxiously. Just one more step and I'm out of here!

Another door slammed, down at the far end of the hall. "Ah, you did find her!" Aunt Eloise, dressed in the slimmest of robes, carrying what appeared to be a wet washcloth over her eye. Her high heels clattered on the parquet floor. As she came closer Lucy changed her mind. It was an ice pack the woman was carrying, not a washcloth.

"They just came in," Jim Proctor said. "You should have stayed in the bathroom, Eloise. Does the eye feel any better?"

"I think you ought to send that little monster away to a boarding school," Aunt Eloise said, and punctuated the sentence with a dry sob. Not very well done, Lucy told herself. If that's the best she can do at crying this woman is a failure.

"And what's *she* doing here?" The sobs rose frantically. There might have been tears, but an ice pack seriously inhibits crying, Lucy thought. The act is a little overdone. I must remember that some time.

"She brought Maude back," Jim Proctor explained. His low voice seemed to throb with sympathy for the thin blonde. He extended an arm toward her, and Eloise slipped into the offered shelter.

"My eye is swelling," Eloise complained. "And there's the Cartwright dinner this evening. You have to *do* something, James."

"I'm going to," he snapped impatiently. "Sit down over there, Eloise. I'll call the doctor in a minute. He can surely do something for your eye."

"You should be so lucky," Lucy muttered. The increasing cosiness of the little love scene was turning her stomach. "Doctors don't make house calls for black eyes. It takes a little something more."

"I don't want to listen to her," Eloise moaned as she moved back into the shadow of Jim's shoulder. "Send her away."

"Er—Miss Borden, I thank you for returning my daughter to me. I would like to talk to you about all this—perhaps a little later? But my fiancée, my daughter and I need to have a little family conversation. Would you mind?"

"I would mind very much." Lucy stamped her little foot. It made a very satisfactory bang. "I don't intend to leave until this is all straightened out."

"Well, really!" Eloise gasped. "Just who in the world do you think you are?"

"I'm just the nosy neighbor who's going to stand by until this is all unraveled, or until the police come." Lucy pulled herself up to her feet and brushed her dress down.

"Oh, please," Maude whimpered. "I don't want him to get mad. I don't——"

"Chin up," Lucy commanded. "Bullies have to be met on their own ground." She stuck her little chin out for emphasis. "Just stand fast."

"Yeah, sure," the child moaned. Lucy could see that her supporting cast was about to fade away, so she hurried.

"Mr. Proctor, why did you throw alcohol all over this child's back?"

"Got some in my eye too," Maude contributed. "It hurts a bunch!"

"Throw alcohol at my child?" His voice almost went through the roof. Lucy swore that she heard a flutter of wings up in the rafters of the high ceiling.

"Throw things at my child?"

"At your child," Lucy managed to repeat. "Child abuse. A serious crime in this country."

"What in the world are you yammering about?" he roared.

Her face flushed, Lucy moved across the room and roared right back at him. "Threw something at the child. And into her eye," she hastened to amend. "All over her back, and scared her half to death. What about that, Mr. Proctor?"

"Oh, no," Maude groaned and came stiffly around the outside of the group. "Not my dad. Not him. Please, not him!"

"Just stay out of it," Lucy urged her. "I'll handle this——"

"It's a fine excuse," Jim Proctor said. His voice had come down from thunderstorm level. "But it won't do. What I want to know is what happened to Eloise's eye. Maude?"

The little girl looked around the circle of adult eyes, and sighed. "I hit her," she said.

"See?" Eloise said excitedly. "See? She's even brazen enough to confess!"

"Just a minute." Proctor held up his hand for quiet. "There's something wrong here," he said. Maude lifted her little chin. Lucy almost swallowed and choked herself. Eloise became very quiet. Proctor went down on one knee in front of his daughter, eye to eye, nose to nose.

"Why?" he coaxed softly. "Why did you hit her?"

The girl hesitated, looked over at Lucy, and then moaned, "Because I didn't want to eat the lousy lunch, and she threw a whole glass of that stuff she drinks, and some of it got in my eye, and I couldn't get it out, and she picked up another glass of that stuff and I run."

So there, Lucy told herself. Right target, wrong horse. Me and my big mouth. *He* didn't abuse the child. My name is going to be mud around these parts for months to come! So it was Eloise who did it?

"It's hard to believe that your aunt would do that," Proctor said, still in that silky soft voice. Lucy moved quickly around to the back of Maude. The child was still wearing the soft bath towel off her shoulders. Gently she peeled the towel away, and then threw Maude's stained blouse down on the floor. The child shivered, either in fear or from the cold.

"Turn around," Lucy said. Maude obeyed. Proctor touched her with a single finger, brought that finger to his nose, and drew in his breath in a sibilant sigh. "Brandy," he spat.

"It may be hard to believe," Lucy said, "but somebody gave her some terrible dose of it. Look how red her eye is. That has to be washed out!"

One of the guards came out into the hall from the living room. "Doctor's at the door," he said. And not a moment afterward Dr. Walters came in, swinging his ancient bag. Somewhat under eighty, stooped and gray, the doctor had long since closed his practice, but did occasionally make house calls. He went directly to the girl and twirled her around.

"Nasty," he muttered. "A little ice on the eye to stop the swelling. An eye cup to wash it out with. Some funky pills in case of infection. If it was an accident somebody ought to be a darn sight more careful. If it wasn't I have to report this to the police."

Proctor climbed back up to his feet. "It was an accident, Doc. I'll see that it never happens again. Thank you for coming."

"But—isn't he going to look at *my* eye?" Eloise asked.

Proctor looked down at the woman for a long frigid moment. "Goodbye, Eloise," he said bleakly.

"But—but we were going to be married very soon," she sputtered.

"Goodbye, Eloise. I've never hit a woman before. Don't give me reason to break my record."

"The girl," the doctor reminded them. "A place to lie down, a bug-hunting pill, a little something to put her to sleep, and someone to watch her until morning."

"Damn you all!" Eloise screamed. "A whole bunch of losers, all of you. It wouldn't have worked anyway, but there was all that money——"

"Goodbye, Eloise." He motioned to one of his men, who came over and took Eloise by the arm, not too gently, and escorted her, still screaming, down the hall.

"I'll take care of Maude." Lucy took the girl's hand and they started down the hall together. Jim Proctor motioned for one of the guards to accompany them. Eloise was still screaming faintly in the distance.

Jim Proctor dropped down into one of the delicate chairs and crammed his big hands into the pockets of his shorts. "How could I have been so wrong?" he sighed.

"It happens," the doctor said. "Now, a few facts for my report?"

"It doesn't hurt so much after that pill," Maude said drowsily. She was stretched out on her stomach on the huge canopied bed in her own room.

"Good. Now remember, don't rub your eye. That's what the little pad is for, to keep you from rubbing it."

"I'm awful glad you was here, Lucy. I was scared. I don't think I've ever seen my dad so mad, not in all my life. You was very brave to talk to him like that!"

"If you swear not to squeal on me," Lucy said, "I'll tell you a secret. I was so scared that I couldn't run.

My legs would just not go!'' She capped the bottle of liquid the doctor had left behind. "There, now. Hungry?''

There was no answer from the bed. The little girl was asleep. "And thank heaven for you,'' Lucy whispered as she went around the bed to a huge armchair by the window, and sank into it. She was half-asleep herself. It had been a long night, she had risen early to meet the builder, and the emotional strain had built and built and built. Both her eyes were almost closed when the creaking door pulled her back to wakefulness. Jim Proctor was stealing gently into the room.

He found her by the dim sparkle of the night-light plugged into a wall socket. "She's asleep,'' Lucy reported.

"I know. I need to talk to you.''

"I need to apologize to you,'' she interrupted. "I thought—I don't know why I thought that *you* had done it.''

"Thanks a lot,'' he grumbled as he moved a chair over beside hers.

"Well, of course you didn't do it,'' Lucy hurried to say. It was hard to see him. The curtains were drawn, the night-light was weak, and he seemed to be some sort of somber shadow as he sank into the chair.

There was just enough light for her to see the drawn expression on his face, the furrows that ran down both sides of his nose.

"I tried to protect her,'' he said softly. "I really tried.''

"I know you did." Her hand, without her permission, moved over to the arm of his chair and patted his wrist.

"Her mother was a mess," he murmured. "I thought—hell, I thought I could take care of her myself, but look how wrong I've been. That was a lucky scare, that was."

"Scare? What scare?" Lucy barely managed to suppress her little shriek of surprise.

"Last summer," he said dully. "The bank business was going from bad to worse. When my brother had his nervous breakdown I had to come and try to glue the bank together."

"You mean you weren't always the—banker?"

"Not me," he said, and she could see his teeth form a grin, even in the semidarkness. "It's always been the family bank, but there's been my father to run it, and my older brother to step into his shoes—so I've been living the life of a rover, so to speak. Including a tour in the navy, a spot of commercial flying—things like that."

"And—all this is what you called picking up the pieces?"

"Just so." He sighed and shifted his weight. "I guess you might include my wife in that too. Once the good times were over—I used to make twice as much money doing test flights as I do now as a banker. Well, once my wife saw the handwriting on the wall she packed her bag and took off. In the middle of the winter, heading north, mind you, with the snow higher than that. She went right off the bridge at the Penobscot River. The sheriff's report said her blood-alcohol level was twice the normal limit.''

"And Maude? She was hurt?"

"Maude? My wife never ever gave the kid a thought. She left Maude all alone in our house in Newton, and took off for the wild blue yonder. All her so-called friends were having a winter-wild party up at one of the winter resorts. What friends.''

"But about Maude?"

"Oh, as usual, I came home late.'' Lucy leaned toward him, feeling the bite of his sarcasm—against himself. "Dear old Dad, zooming into the drive at ten o'clock at night, to find Maude and her little bear huddled in the closet, shivering. She's been afraid of the dark ever since! I'm never going to let that happen again, Lucy Borden. No matter what the price, I'm never going to let that happen again! I never dreamed that Eloise would—hell, she always treated Maude and me as if we were royalty. And now look. I'm not much of a judge of women, Lucy.''

"Don't think about it.'' To her surprise, Lucy found that her hand still rested on top of his. "You weren't entirely responsible.''

"I *need* to think about it,'' he grumbled. "I can't help but think that my plan is all right. I've just got the wrong woman. And by the end of the month I have to go to Washington. It looks as if the whole banking system is going to collapse. We're all in a lot of trouble from lousy real-estate loans.''

He shook himself, the way a big dog would do to dry himself after the rain.

"Well," he murmured again, "so what do you think?"

Lucy shook herself as well. Too many real-estate loans? To many *bad* real-estate loans! What do I think? Perhaps there was something he had said that she had missed. Anything was possible. "I—don't remember," she sighed. "Would you—what do I think about what?"

His big shadow leaned in her direction. She shrank back in her chair, clutching at the arms. "Well, I told you. I have to protect Maude, but we're facing a banking crisis and I have to get to a meeting at the Treasury Department. I thought it would work out. I would marry Eloise. She would look after Maude— and, who knows, a family might have developed?"

Lucy pulled her hand back, only to find it quickly trapped by his massive fingers.

"But no," he continued rambling. "It could only have worked if Eloise had been as nice a woman as you are. Instead, I almost married a crazy—another crazy. So there it is."

"It is?"

"Yes." A very final *yes*, as if he had come to some momentous conclusion.

"I——"

"No doubt about it." He stood up, and pulled her after him. "No doubt about it, Lucastra Borden. The church is all laid on, the flowers have been ordered, the guests invited. Everything's ready. One week from Tuesday morning at eleven o'clock down at the Congregational Church. You know where that is?''

"I suppose I could find it," she whispered. His fingers tightened on her right hand. "I've only been a member of the parish for sixteen years."

"Good," he added and started to drag her toward the door.

"Good what?" she repeated as they stepped out into the hall.

"Why, I've explained all that."

"Not quite," she sighed. He released her fingers and shifted both hands to her shoulders. "You left out something. What does all this have to do with me?"

He stared down at her, astonished. "Why, you're responsible for all this mess," he told her, "so one week from Tuesday you're going to marry me, and look after Maude. I'd better get stirring, I still have a lot of things to take care of."

Yes, I'll bet you do, Lucy told herself as she folded her arms across her chest and watched him vanish down the hall. I'm going to marry you one week from Tuesday? That'll be a cold morning in summer, Mr. Proctor.

CHAPTER FIVE

"HI THERE, little lady." Lucy stopped at the hail. Her builder-in-chief was pursuing her as she came around the side of the house.

"Hi, yourself. Everything going all right?"

"Not exactly, ma'am. There seems to be another problem that would require——"

"Don't tell me. More money?"

"Ayup. Termites. Under the back porch. The whole shebang will have to come down if you really want a wheelchair exit for the old lady. It'll go—oh—another four thousand dollars?"

"Which we don't have?"

"Which we don't have," he agreed mournfully.

"Money seems to flow like water around here," she grumbled. "No other way to fix it?"

"Nope."

Lucy stood there in the sand, her bare feet spread slightly, her hands on hips, nibbling at her lower lip. Two weeks ago she would have fainted at the idea. Now—another four thousand that we don't have— what the hey? It didn't seem so tremendous a blow. Bad, but not impossible. But maybe, she told herself, I shouldn't have bought this new bathing suit. Fifty-five dollars for something to swim in? But it did look nice, and it had boosted her morale by a thousand per cent.

She turned to look up the beach, to where *his* house sat brooding in the morning sun. I'm going to marry him? What kind of a fool does he think I am? So I'll borrow some more money from his bank. Maybe that way he'll discover that wives can be expensive! The thought was so delightful that she reversed course, went back into the house, and called her favorite banker.

"More money?" Angie asked when they met in the kitchen over a hot cup of tea.

"More money," Lucy said, sighing. "They don't seem worried down at the bank. At least my loan officer says so. Incidentally, he asked after you. Somehow he had heard that you were in bad shape, and he was concerned."

"How polite," Angie said. "And how strange. I don't know him from a hill of beans. Can it be there are a few polite people in the younger generation?"

"If there are, I've missed them," Lucy said, and then changed the subject. "If I had the nerve I'd borrow all the money he has in his fool bank, and then laugh at him when he comes around for repayment."

"Him?"

"You know. Jim Proctor. Jimbo." A pause to reflect, with both her elbows on the table, as Angie Moore and those pale blue eyes measured her up and down.

"Thinking a lot about Mr. Proctor, aren't you, girl? What is it? Does he remind you a lot of Mark?"

"Dear Lord, no." Lucy's hand went unconsciously to her cheek, which was as red as a fire storm. "He's nothing like Mark. Nothing. Mark was taller and lighter—and better mannered. Mark was a gentleman to the teeth."

"And Jimbo?"

"Wide and square and—crude sometimes." And more powerful and direct. Mark you could cajole. Jim couldn't be diverted for love or money!

"Ah. Jim's the lion, and you don't mind teasing him? Not asking for too much trouble, are we?"

"Of course I am," Lucy snapped. "And I don't know what to do about it. He still insists he's going to marry me. What can you do with a man like that? I've told him three times that it wasn't ever going to happen, and he just laughs. Well, I'll show him. My swimming school starts today. Fourteen girls—and Maude, of course."

"Does he know about it?"

"About what? About the swimming school? No, I guess he doesn't, but then it's none of his business, is it?"

"In a manner of speaking, yes, it is," Angie returned. "You're building it with his money, even though he doesn't know it."

"Borrowed money doesn't have an owner," Lucy insisted. "Borrowed. Legally, at that! Do you think this suit is perhaps a little——?"

.

"Not a bit," Angie said, smirking. "If I were only forty years younger I'd wear it myself. Ah—here they come."

"Here they come." Lucy sighed. Her tea was too hot to drink, and she needed it so badly. She walked out on the front porch to greet her first class, to introduce herself, and to settle the rules. Not one of the parents made a move to inspect the place. In fact, two of the girls were delivered by chauffeurs. Their parents had found a place to store their loving daughters and were only too eager to have them off their hands. Out of sight, out of mind, so to speak. By nine-thirty they were all in the water as Lucy segregated them into smaller groups by their abilities. And then to work.

The morning passed quickly. By eleven-thirty most of the girls were stretched out on the beach, out of breath. The new bathroom was not yet finished; Lucy opted to send them home well salted. The house bustled with their noise. In fact, the whole neighborhood rocked. But it was sweet music to Lucy. As she waved goodbye to the last child her mind was running in the fast lane.

"Fifteen dollars a week each," she said elatedly to Angie Moore.

"Two hundred and ten dollars a week for the whole," said that worthy, who was faster with arithmetic than the average woman.

"Wow! I think I'll go spend some of it!"

"You'd better hold off until you find out how much your loan repayment will come to," Angie advised.

"Repayment? I've hardly got it," Lucy said gloomily. "Repayment so soon?"

"That's the way it works, love."

Disenchanted, Lucy went off upstairs to shower and change into something more utilitarian. Maude was already in the shower, singing her heart away.

Lucy knocked on the door. "Save me some hot water," she shouted. The shower sounds came to an end, and in a moment the girl stuck her head through the doorjamb.

"There ain't any hot water," she announced. "Mr. Henderson, he said that——"

"I'd better go talk to him myself." Maude scooted back into the shower as Lucy wandered back downstairs. Angie was just hanging up the telephone. There was a disturbed look on her face.

"Something?"

"Nothing important," Angie reported. "My annuity check just came in. I managed to get hold of my bookie. I put down a little something on the first at Aqueduct."

"And made a bundle?"

"Bite your tongue, girl. They've just started the third race, and my horse hasn't come in yet!"

With that bit of good news behind her, Lucy went out into the back yard, where everything was quiet. Mr. Henderson was sitting on the back stoop, a half-eaten sandwich in his hand. He made a motion to get up when she appeared. She waved him back, and sat down beside him.

"Lotta fun them kids is havin'," he commented. "Makes me wish I weren't so old myself."

"Bring a suit and have yourself a dip," she commented.

"Don't believe I've actually got a bathing suit," he admitted. "Couldn't call it no swimsuit. I never learned to swim."

"Haven't got a suit? Living this close to the water?"

"Ayup. Happens a lot around these parts."

A moment of mutual silence as the gulls dive-bombed the beach and screeched at each other, as the waves curtsied in and out, as the sun beat warmly on their heads, as an occasional splash indicated smaller fish trying to evade being selected for dinner by larger ones. The strong, clear smell of the ocean cleaned the air of man's pollutions. Lucy took a deep breath and enjoyed.

"Hot water." Lucy introduced the subject.

"Got the old tank out," he reported. "Put the new one in in a couple of days, we will. Big tank. Biggest I could find anywheres. Now you'll 'scuse me, little lady, I gotta get back to work."

"Me too," Lucy said as she went off hunting for her beach rakes. Her school had accumulated a lot of clutter in just one morning.

About two o'clock in the afternoon Maude came out of the house, and apologized. "You won't believe it, but I fell asleep. I don't know when I've been so tired."

"It's not important." Lucy managed a smile and handed the child a small rake. "But don't let it happen again." Said aggressively, as if correcting a major crime. Maude smiled up at her and they continued the raking.

At four o'clock Jim Proctor turned up. He wore a pair of ragged shorts, and an equally ragged undershirt with a "Harvard Rowing" insignia on it. Both shirt and insignia looked as if they had gone down with the *Titanic* and been resurrected.

"Hard work?" he asked.

"Oh, no," Lucy commented as she straightened up and groaned. "In modern society all the *hard* work is done by men."

"You don't believe that!" Maude exclaimed.

"No, but your daddy does."

"Now wait a minute," he complained. "I don't need you to put words in my mouth, lady. That, by the way, is a very fetching suit. You don't go for the bikini style any more, I take it."

"No, I don't," Lucy snapped. "I don't believe in overexposure."

"So why all this necessity to clean up the beach?"

"Because we got a swimming school," Maude burst out.

"A swimming school?"

"Yes," Lucy agreed. "We've accumulated a number of students, and we're conducting lessons. I need the money."

"Well, now." He swung his daughter up on one hip. Lucy, who had tried the same trick not two hours earlier, was totally impressed. Maude was a solid chunk of little girl—solid. The two teased each other for a moment, while Lucy watched. He finally dropped her to the sand. "I hope you're not charging money for this—no, you wouldn't be *that* stupid."

Lucy felt a little quiver go up her back. Have I missed out on something? How does he know just how stupid I might be? She shook her head, but her fists were clenched tight.

"Why, is there something wrong with charging for services?" she asked. It was difficult to make her voice sound casual.

"No, usually. But this area is all zoned as residential. Nobody can run a commercial business here—that is, without a variance from the board of selectmen."

"Well, that's pretty silly," Maude intervened. "You can't run a swimming school unless you've got ocean. The school has to be where the water is. What's the matter, Lucy? You look so—pale."

"I all of a sudden don't feel so good." Lucy turned on her heel and ran for the house. Maude and her father watched, shaking their heads.

"She works awful hard," Maude told her father.

"Yes, I can see that." He took the child's hand and they ploughed their way up to the other house.

Meanwhile, Lucy just managed to dodge Angie's chair on her way to the bathroom, and didn't return for another fifteen minutes.

"Something you ate?" Angie enquired solicitously.

"Something I heard," Lucy admitted. "He said—oh, Lord, I don't want to remember what he said. How about chicken for dinner?"

Dinner was a disaster. Not that the chicken was poorly prepared, nor because it tasted poorly. It was her stomach that was upset, and her mind that made it so. But Angie Moore, when she was not in one of her seizures, was a cheerful companion. Lucy felt the need to be as cheerful. After all, Angie was a mass of aches and pains, while Lucy only had an upset stomach. So from dinner to the early hour when Angie went to bed was a time of acting. And when all the bedtime requirements were met Lucy sampled the night air, changed into a simple paneled sundress, and went out to walk the beach and commune with her troubles.

It was a sleepy clear night. The moon was just rising over the eastern horizon. The sea birds had retreated to wherever they spent their nights, and the surf had dropped. The soft susurrus of the waves striking the beach finally hypnotized her. Lucy went back up to the massive rock that was her boundary line with That Man's land, leaned back against the stone, and set her mind in neutral.

She had no idea how much time had passed; she was just beginning to feel the cool of the night, but in too much of a daze to go in for a sweater. And it was just at that moment when she felt someone coming up behind her. Not heard. There was not enough sound to penetrate the noise of the wavelets. Just felt.

Mattapoisett was a small town, yet it possessed all the illnesses of any American town. Night time on the beach was really no place for a girl all alone. Not that she felt fear. She was able to separate the various signals of that coming. A presence sprinkled with the odor of after-shave, and that indescribable something that was maleness. Suddenly the warmth of something was thrown around her shoulders. She turned slowly and looked down. A man's jacket, color unknown, because the moon was painting it silver. She snuggled down into it, and then there was an arm around her, warm, comforting, protective. A delicious little shiver ran up and down her spine, and the arm tightened.

"Lucastra?"

"Well, you know it is," she said, sighing. "There's not another girl within a mile. Jim?"

"Well, of course it is. Who else would be hugging you on the beach at this hour of the day?" She made a slight move, and his arm tightened again. "No, this is no time for you to run for cover. Relax."

It was a command, and Lucy was not the sort of woman to respond well to commands. But this was a night out of time, a strange passage which she could not resist. So she relaxed.

There was an infinity of silence. Out in the bay the running lights of a boat popped up, cut across their line of sight, and disappeared. The few night-lights of the city cast a glow down there on their right. He was looking up at the stars. She took the cue and joined him. Somehow she shifted, her head on his shoulder as they searched the constellations.

"Beautiful." His low deep voice caressed her hair.

She relaxed even further, his shoulder and flank supporting her entirely. "Yes. They always are." The hand around her shoulders squeezed again.

"I meant you, Lady Lucastra, not the stars."

It was a surprising compliment, but it left her feeling uncomfortable. She squirmed an inch or two, but could not escape his arm.

"Did no one ever tell you that you're beautiful?"

"Not since my grandmother died."

Another moment or two of silence. "Have you ever been in love?"

A little giggle. "Not recently. I was in love with Harry Tillman, but it didn't last."

A gruffer voice. "Harry Tillman? Does he live around here?"

"Oh, for goodness' sake. We were in the sixth grade together. I haven't seen Harry since—I don't remember. Years and years ago."

"Ah, well, that makes it all right."

He tilted her chin upward, and kissed her fore-head, a gentle persuasive touch of warmth. "I just can't stand competition," he said wryly.

"Competition? I don't understand." But I'll never tell him about Mark!

"Good. We'll just keep it that way." His hand came off her shoulder, and played through her hair. An offshore wind was rising, adding to the confusion. Ordinarily Lucy would have attempted to curb her hair; for this moment she let the wind—and him—have their way.

"And you? Have *you* ever been in love?"

A lengthier pause while he thought it over. Stupid question, she told herself fiercely. Just when every-thing's going so—nicely—you have to open your big mouth and put your foot in it. He's been married. He has a child. Stupid! What could he possibly say?

"I thought I had." Said softly, just barely audible. "But now I think not. It was a terrible mistake. For both of us. She wanted—a different sort of life than I did. I feel terribly guilty now to say it, but when it was over I was—relieved."

Lucy shook herself and stood up. "I'm sorry I snooped," she said. "But it's late, my schoolgirls will come early, and——"

And whatever it was she intended to say flew com-pletely out of her mind. He had turned her to face him, and his lips came down on hers. Still gentle, still persuasive. What to do now? Lucy asked herself. Stand here and absorb, or——? And at that second all choice was taken from her. His arms tightened just the slightest bit around her, his lips demanded, and his sudden fever attacked Lucy's controls, and she was gone.

Gone into that never-never land where people were joined together as one, gone into that melting, merging compulsion where only emotions raged, and self was abandoned to the frantic attack. Gone to where her nerves were all responding in different modes and directions, and where the skies lit up——!

He broke away from her. She could hear his heavy breathing. "What in heaven's name was that?" he demanded. Lucy managed to get her eyes unfocused. The sky had *really* lit up. Someone across the harbor had sent up a white flare.

"Flare," she said. "The Coast Guard Reserve is conducting a night training exercise."

"I'd like to kill them all," he muttered.

So would I, Lucy told herself. Violently and tortuously. Where were we? Whatever happened? Nobody ever told me that kissing men was dangerous to my health.

"You're shivering," he commented.

"Yes..." she stammered. "I—it's getting chilly. I think I'd better go in. There are things to arrange for tomorrow..." And dreams to study and reassess and— he's blown my whole mind! I suppose it's just lust—or whatever they call it these days. But whatever it is, I've got to think this through before I talk to this man again.

"G'night." She whirled around, out of his arms, and ran for her back door.

"Lucy," he called softly, not daring to waken the neighborhood. She ignored it, dived into the house, and rushed upstairs. She spent the rest of the night tossing and turning in her suddenly not so innocent bed.

As for Jim Proctor, he stomped up and down the beach two or three more turns, hoping she might reappear, but after a time it became obvious that the night's delights were over. He mentioned two or three unprintable words, scaled a rock or two into the mocking ocean, and went in to bed. Where he too had difficulty falling asleep.

The sun was in shadows on the fifth day of the swimming school, but neither the pupils nor the teacher were much concerned. The girls were engaged in medley racing when the police car came up.

"Lucy," Mrs. Moore yelled. The back porch had been partially modified so she could ride her wheelchair out into the open. "Lucy! There's a policeman here who needs to—that's him."

The tall uniformed man, following the voices, had come around the side of the house and went walking down the beach. Lucy gave a few instructions to her oldest pupils, who served as monitors, and waded up out of the surf.

"You wanted to see me, Officer?"

"Well—er—yes." He was a tall black-haired man, younger than Lucy herself, built like a full back on some football team. "If you are the owner of this place, that is."

"I am. For the moment."

"For the moment?"

"Yes. The bank owns a part of all this, and if they foreclose, why—well, that doesn't matter. As of the moment I am the owner of record."

"And this is a private school you are conducting?" He had a checklist on his clipboard, and for every answer he made an entry.

"Yes to both."

"Ma'am?"

"I mean yes, it's a private school, and yes, I am conducting it, but no, you can't join because it's only for girls, you know."

"I—er—see." There evidently was no place on his checklist for such an answer, but he looked just to be sure. "No, I didn't want to join your school. Do you——?" His tongue came out to the corner of his mouth as he checked his list again. "Is this a profit-making school?"

"It's hard to tell." Lucy shook her head sorrowfully. "It was *meant* to be a profit-making school, but it isn't yet, and I suspect it might not be for the rest of the season." Lucy looked around hastily for some backup, but for once her builder was not in sight. She sighed disgustedly and turned back to the policeman.

That's one important thing about any man, she told herself. He's never available when you need him!

Back to his clipboard, with a disgusted expression on his face. Then he swallowed and put his paper behind his back. "Are you charging money for these girls to come and swim?"

"I am. Indeed I am. Not enough, though." She was distracted for a moment. Maude had come out of the water to listen, and now she was yelling at somebody up by her own house.

"Do you have a permit to operate such a business here, ma'am?"

"Permit? I wish you wouldn't call me ma'am. I'm not that old. Lucy is my name. Lucy Borden."

"I know your name—ma'am." The young policeman was completely disoriented by this time. Perhaps it had something to do with Lucy's new bathing suit, a which fitted her like a second skin. Its color didn't do him any good, either. It was beige, the same color as Lucy's well-tanned skin, and it was low cut, giving a very attractive view to men of his age. When she breathed it made a deep impression on an impressionable male. "I know your name," he repeated. "You went to school with my brother."

"Oh? Who was——?"

"Look, lady, I didn't come to let you lead me down the garden path. Do you have a license from the town to operate this school in a residential area? We have a complaint."

NO RISK, NO OBLIGATION TO BUY...NOW OR EVER!

GUARANTEED

PLAY "ROLL A DOUBLE" AND GET AS MANY AS FIVE FREE GIFTS!

HERE'S HOW TO PLAY:

1. Peel off label from front cover. Place it in space provided at right. With a coin, carefully scratch off the silver dice. This makes you eligible to receive two or more free books, and possibly another gift, depending on what is revealed beneath the scratch-off area.

2. Send back this card and you'll receive brand-new Harlequin Presents® novels. These books have a cover price of $2.99 each, but they are yours to keep absolutely free.

3. There's no catch. You're under no obligation to buy anything. We charge nothing – ZERO – for your first shipment. And you don't have to make any minimum number of purchases – not even one!

4. The fact is thousands of readers enjoy receiving books by mail from the Harlequin Reader Service® months before they're available in stores. They like the convenience of home delivery and they love our discount prices!

5. We hope that after receiving your free books you'll want to remain a subscriber. But the choice is yours – to continue or cancel, anytime at all! So why not take us up on our invitation, with no risk of any kind. You'll be glad you did!

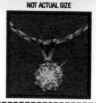

THE HARLEQUIN READER SERVICE®: HERE'S HOW IT WORKS

Accepting free books puts you under no obligation to buy anything. You may keep the books and gift and return the shipping statement marked "cancel." If you do not cancel, about a month later we will send you 6 additional novels, and bill you just $2.24 each plus 25¢ delivery and applicable sales tax, if any.* That's the complete price, and – compared to cover prices of $2.99 each – quite a bargain! You may cancel at any time, but if you choose to continue, every month we'll send you 6 more books, which you may either purchase at the discount price...or return at our expense and cancel your subscription.

*Terms and prices subject to change without notice. Sales tax applicable in N.Y.

NO POSTAGE
NECESSARY
IF MAILED
IN THE
UNITED STATES

BUSINESS REPLY MAIL
FIRST CLASS MAIL   PERMIT NO. 717   BUFFALO, NY

POSTAGE WILL BE PAID BY ADDRESSEE

HARLEQUIN READER SERVICE
3010 WALDEN AVE
PO BOX 1867
BUFFALO NY 14240-9952

If offer card is missing, write to : The Harlequin Reader Service, 3010 Walden Ave., P.O. Box 1867, Buffalo, NY 14269-1867.

Lucy glared up at him. It was against the law, she knew, to set your dog at a policeman. Besides, she didn't have a dog. The man had brown eyes, and with every closure of his lids as he blinked she could see a dollar bill disappear. As he stared at her, and she stared back with open mouth, two hundred dollars had already disappeared down the drain. "Help," she muttered, almost under her breath.

There were no guardian angels in the neighborhood. "So what does all that mean?" Her voice was barely strong enough to reach him.

"Why, I'm giving you notification," the officer said. "You are in violation of the town zoning ordinance. You have to shut down. Should you care to appeal you have to petition the board of selectmen, and ask them to grant you a variance."

"You—don't think I could run my school until the board meets? I know it takes some considerable time for them to—no, huh?" The officer was shaking his head from side to side. Smiling, cheerful, but giving her a positive negative. She glared at him. "I'll bet if you were your brother you'd arrange it for me."

"If I were my brother?"

"You remember. The one that went to school with me."

"Well, perhaps he would. Unfortunately he's in Saudi Arabia, drilling oil wells."

"I couldn't even finish the morning? It's just another hour, and——" And maybe I might be struck by an attack of common sense, she told herself. But the young man smiled again.

"Don't see anything wrong in that," he said as he made one last check on his little list. "I'll be coming by this way at two o'clock, and you'd better be shut down by then."

"Yes," she said sadly. "Yes, indeed." There were lots of other things she wanted to say to him, nasty things, but this was obviously not the place. And a girl needed to keep on the right side of young policemen at all times. "Thank you," she added.

He shook his head at her again, and grinned. Perhaps he would have said something, but evidently something was going on to the back of her. He tipped the peak of his uniform cap and waited patiently.

"Having a little trouble, are we?" A deep voice, loaded with laughter, from just behind her left shoulder. She looked around at him. Jim Proctor. And at such an embarrassing time!

"No," she protested under her breath. "Not you."

"Yup. Me." He came up behind her. There was an "oooh" sound from all the girls, who had come up to form a semicircle around them. Lucy blushed.

"I'm Mr. Proctor, the banker," he told the officer. "Now just what are you accusing my fiancée of?"

Lucy started to object. He hugged her tightly against him, applying enough pressure to send her a message. She read it as "Shut up, little lady, while we men settle things!" It made her angrier, but she complied.

"Well, now," the officer said. "We have a complaint that the—your fiancée is running a commercial business in a zoned residential area."

"Who would make a fool complaint like that?" Proctor said. "The old biddy across the street?"

The old biddy across the street? Lucy bent to one side to see around her house. There *was* an old house across the street, so far away from the street that she could barely see the chimneys.

"Mrs. Chase," the policeman confirmed. "Noises, girls running around half-naked—and she slipped on her stepladder when she climbed up on it to see what was going on. Through the dormer window, you see. Sprained her ankle, she said. Wants to sue you for damages." The two men exchanged smiles, a secret password of the male animal, Lucy told herself, and bit her tongue to keep from saying something of the sort aloud.

"But of course, Mr. Proctor, there *is* a legal problem. We maintain the zoning ordinances very carefully. If your—lady—wants to run this business she has to get a waiver from the town. And until then——"

"Now let's not be hasty," Proctor said. "You must realize that this is not exactly a business. It's more like a sports endeavor. And coupled with the fact that Lucy is keeping more than a dozen of these girls out of some other trouble. I'm sure you recognize one or two of them?"

"Yes. Three of them, for a fact. Rich fathers, spoiled kids. Yeah, I hadn't thought of that. Nevertheless——"

"So, then, the truth is she isn't really conducting a business *per se*. Correct?"

The policeman nodded.

"So there's no need to shut her down so suddenly—because she'll apply for a variance immediately anyway. And you wouldn't want to turn any of these hellcats back to the streets..." He gestured at the girls surrounding them.

"No," the policeman agreed. "Wouldn't want them back on the streets. But it's only for a day or so, you understand." He tucked his little notebook back into his pocket, gave Proctor a satisfied smile, and headed back to his patrol car.

Lucy watched him disappear around the corner of the house, and then she turned back to Jim. "But what does it all mean?"

"It means you're breaking the law six ways from Sunday," he said. "You not only don't have a permit to operate a private school, but you haven't paid the tax that goes with it. Surprise me. Tell me you *have* already."

"I haven't already," she muttered. And then, with more confidence, louder, "You didn't expect me to surprise you, so why are you going on like that? What am I going to do now? I do have a license, you know."

"From the town?"

"Well, not exactly. From the Red Cross. That makes it sort of legal, doesn't it?"

"I'm afraid you'll have to close down for a time," he said. "Or go noncommercial."

"Noncommercial?"

"Yeah. Don't charge anything for a day or so. I know I've got a good thing going here for Maude, and I'll check around among some of the other parents for support, and in the meantime the bank owns a lawyer, and I'll whisper in his shell pink ear and he'll get up and do something about it. Right?"

"Lord, what a narrow-minded world," Lucy said. "It doesn't even sound honest!"

"But you don't want to lose your school, do you? I talked to Angie a few minutes ago, and she says you really need the money."

"All right, girls," Lucy snapped. "This is a school, not a gossip corner. Everybody back into the water." She clapped her hands and the girls, all wearing mile-wide smiles, dashed for the water. "You too, Miss Proctor. Shoo."

"But I wanna——"

"Go while you're able," her father interrupted. Maude took one look, stuck out her tongue at him, and ran. "Now, you really need the money be-cause——"

"I don't think that's any of your——"

"Lucy!"

"Well, I don't, Mr. Proctor. And I don't intend to marry you, and I don't intend to——" The last statement ended in a squeak of alarm as he swept her up in his arms and thoroughly kissed her. She was still gasping for breath when he put her down again.

"Now look," he said, "I don't mind a little bit of independence now and again. But sometimes, Lucy, you really do try my patience. Now why do you need money at this particular moment?"

It almost came out. So that I can pay off your darn loan, she wanted to say, but dared not. Why try to tame the tiger? If he found out that his own bank was loaning me all the money to fix my house he'd undoubtedly go right through the roof! And, she told herself, I don't like the way he's treating me, but I can afford to get even later on! And so, letting caution be her guide, she muttered, "I have a few bills I've accumulated."

"If that's all it is," he said, "you could have just said so. Give me a list and I'll have my secretary pay it off. Part of the wedding price, so to speak."

Lucy threw up her hands. "You just don't listen," she snapped. "I'm not going to marry you, and you can't buy me, so there won't be any wedding prices, or Oh, you infuriate me!"

"Yes, that's what I hoped to do." He gave her one of his patented "treat the little girl nicely" smiles. If he pats me on the head, Lucy thought, I'm going to— And that was the moment he patted her on the head. Unfortunately, he accompanied the pat by nibbling at her ear, and then kissing her again. Thoroughly. It drove whatever she had intended completely out of her mind. He stepped back to admire his handiwork, leaving her standing in the wind, swaying, dazed.

"Yes," he said unctuously. "That'll do for today."

"What are you talking about?" she yelled after him as he turned and walked back up the beach.

"Don't forget," he called, "five days till the wedding!"

She wanted very much to run after him, to trip him up in the sand, to—— A very lurid thought followed. A thought that had no right to be wandering around loose in her mind. She shrugged it off, but not too easily, and then went back down the beach. After all, she still had fourteen pupils waiting for their teacher.

Damn the man!

It took some time after the girls had gone before Lucy could explain it all to Angie. "So I have to start repaying on the loan by next week," she said, sighing. "It's an awful lot of money, and payments are due every month, and——"

"I know it's all very complex," Angie said, and her pale blue eyes were twinkling, "but I think there must be a simple solution. At least for the first payment."

"Easy?"

Angie reached for the telephone, and paused for a moment. "Of course, easy. His bank is willing to lend you money, no?"

Lucy nodded, wide eyed, as the old lady started to dial a number.

"Then go back to the bank and borrow enough money to pay for the first two or three loan repayments, my dear."

Lucy was still standing there with her mouth open when the party Angie was calling answered her telephone. "Abigail? Abigail Chase? This is Angie Moore calling. Look, you ancient bag of bones, how dare you file a complaint against my Lucy?" The old lady winked at Lucy as she listened to the barrage from the other end of the telephone.

"Well, I wouldn't want you to be exposed to such loose living, Abigail, although I'm one of several in the neighborhood who can remember back to World War II, and all the funny business that went on down on the beach about you and that—what was his name? Remember that?"

Another barrage from the other end, until Angie Moore interrupted. "You wouldn't forget, Abigail, that I own the mortgage on your house? And a big mortgage it is, isn't it? You could pack up and be gone quickly, my dear. The town has some lovely apartment houses for the elderly. One room and a bath. You'd love them. And—oh? Well, I think if you withdraw your complaint things might come about. Yes, goodbye." She set the telephone down on its base and smiled. "And so you see, Lucastra, you have *some* friends in the neighborhood."

"But to borrow more money?" Lucy had both hands to her hot, blushing cheeks. "Isn't that dishonest?"

"Not at all," Angie retorted. "The old Christian law considered any interest charges over six per cent as being usury. Bankers deserve everything they get! Have some dinner, love, and get to bed. Tomorrow will be a busy borrowing day."

So Lucy Borden stumbled upstairs for a quick bath and then dived into her bed. And all night long Angie's statement ran through her mind, but with a different connotation. Bankers deserve everything they get! Is it possible that Jim Proctor might get me?

CHAPTER SIX

LUCY BORDEN woke up the following morning from the middle of a horrible dream. Jim Proctor had been leaning over her bed, his face twisted in a terrible sneer. "Money," he repeated over and over again. "Money—or else! Nobody cheats on *my* bank." Lucy sat up in bed, and forced her eyes to open. One moment she had been fast asleep, the next she was sitting up in bed. Bewildered, she muttered, "Money. Borrow money?" Then, after a confused moment, "Or else?"

And then another rambling thought. "How in the world did Angie own a mortgage on that great pile of a house across the street?" She blinked her eyes, trying to get the sand out of them. "Money," she muttered. "I've got to get some money."

Angie Moore was just stirring downstairs. Lucy helped her up, helped her to dress, and then wheeled her out to the kitchen. "Breakfast?" she suggested. Angie gave her a big smile, somewhat perkier than she had shown in the past two weeks.

"Ham and eggs," she ordered. "Coffee."

"Angie—you know the doctor said you weren't to drink coffee."

"Insolent young pup, that doctor. What does he know? Coffee!"

"So coffee." Lucy sighed and shrugged. Breakfast was delayed. The cook was walking like a zombie. With edibles on the table, and two large sips of hot coffee under her belt, her brain began to function.

"Mortgages," she said, her mouth half full of scrambled eggs.

"Mortgages?"

"You said to that lady on the telephone that you held a mortgage on her house, Angie. And all the time I thought you were broke!"

"Well, it's true, child. I *am* broke. That is to say, I don't have any money. But I have a sackful of papers that I've been accumulating over the past twenty-five years. Anything that was money I spent. Everything else I just threw in the closet."

"But——"

"You're curious? Why don't you have a look? They're all stored in that big trunk next to my bed. I don't think they're worth much, but I meant you to have them all anyway."

"You wouldn't mind?"

"Not a bit. Go right ahead."

"You're not curious?"

"Not a bit. There's nothing more boring than a trunkful of papers. They gather dust, you know, and that bothers my asthma."

"I—maybe some rainy day," Lucy said. "There's no swimming class today, and I have to be at the bank promptly at nine o'clock."

"You'd better run, love."

Maude came bouncing in at that moment, full of sunshine and devilry. "I'm gonna baby-sit you, Angie," the little girl announced. "And you'd better hurry, Lucy. He's just walking around playing Napoleon, giving orders like crazy. I don't *think* he's going to the bank."

"What a lovely child," Angie Moore said. The girl giggled.

"My father says I'm a saucy baggage," Maude said. "What does that mean?"

"Just that he loves you very much," the old lady responded. "Now, what are we going to do while you're grandmother-sitting?"

Lucy took that as ample assurance that all would be well on the home front, so she started out, heading for the bank. In her lightweight green tracksuit with the orange stripe down the legs, and her hair in a ponytail, she looked like some sixteen-year-old, starting down Ned's Point Road at a jog. The world was full of summer sunshine. She had not gone more than ten feet toward the town center before a car pulled up behind her, and a trumpet horn blared. Lucy jumped.

"Don't do that," she muttered as she turned to look inside the silver mirror of the Cadillac. And then, much louder, "Don't do that! You scared me out of what little wits I have left!"

"Going my way?" Jim Proctor, with expansive smile and banker's uniform.

"Which way are you going?" she asked cautiously.

"To Town Hall."

"No—I'm not going that way!" she exclaimed. She had walked hardly any distance, but already she was short of breath, and her heart was beating madly. It couldn't possibly be physical?

"And if I had said I was going north to the highway?"

"No. I'm not going that way either—thank you."

He leaned across and threw open the passenger-side door. "Lucy Borden, don't you tease at me. If you're not going in either of those directions there's no place else to go in this town except into the harbor. Now stop giving me a hard time, and get in!"

"I will not. And you can't make me!" And that ought to set him right, she told herself. Just because he's big and scrawny there's no reason to—— Why is he getting out of the car?

"Jim Proctor! Don't you dare——" He had already come around the hood of the parked car. She backed up a pace or two. "You can't park your car in the middle of the road!"

"Oh, I can't? And I don't dare? And I can't make you? Hah!" It was the sort of "hah" that translated into "oh, yeah?" and presently she found herself swinging and squirming in his arms, tucked into his chest just below his chin. It was, in fact, a very comfortable place to be. For a moment Lucy savored it, and then she remembered her goal. There is no way, she told herself, that I can walk into *his* bank and borrow some more of *his* money. Not after the way he treated me on my first visit. When was that? Years ago? Or really only last week?

"Put me down, you monstrous man," she muttered into the collar of his suit coat.

"What was that?"

"I said *put me down*!"

"Yes, I heard that. Did you notice we're gathering a crowd?"

"That's because you've parked square in the middle of the road, and nobody can get by on either side, idiot!"

"Ah. Kindly love words." He chuckled, and tickled her just under her rib. She bounced up but not out of his arms.

"I hate that sort of thing," she said. "Hate it. Add that to your list, Mr. What's-Your-Name!"

"Proctor," he said patiently. "Just keep trying, Lucy, and my name will come to you. After all, it'll be your name too! And Maude's as well."

"Never. Do you hear that? Never. If I live to be a thousand years old I'll never marry you, you——!" Once again he had done the impossible: closed her mouth by the simple expedient of kissing her.

August was not the busiest month in the world. A small crowd had already gathered. At the kissing bit the audience responded. Half of them, all women, applauded. The other half, all men, cheered.

Lucy, with her face a bright red, struggled fruit-lessly to escape. "Look what you're doing to me," she spat in his ear. "They all know me! I'm totally embarrassed."

"Totally?"

"Yes, totally. Put me down this instant!"

Instead he gripped her all the more tightly, and took a deep breath. "Ladies and gentlemen," he bellowed, and paused for effect. He had a very large voice. It could probably be heard all the way across the harbor, Lucy thought. And beyond. Down to Brandt's Point, perhaps. She just could not stop herself from shivering. About twenty-five people stopped in their casual morning pursuits and turned around to watch.

"I am informed," he bellowed, "that most of you know Miss Lucy Borden, and may be embarrassed to see her so thoroughly kissed in public."

"Stop it," she whispered as she tried to hide out of sight.

"Well, let me assure you," he bellowed on, "that this is all perfectly moral and decent and legal. Next Tuesday Lucy is going to do me the honor of marrying me in the Congregational Church just up the street here, on Church Street. And I want you, all who can, to attend the wedding. And the reception thereafter, on the beach behind my house. Refreshments will be served in large quantities. Be sure to tell your friends!"

Another burst of applause broke through the crowd. Jim set Lucy down on her feet, but still treasured her to his chest. "Why, you're crying," he said gently, and teased a tear away with one big thumb. "There, now, Lucy, there's no need to cry. From here on in I'll be protecting you from all comers. Come on, now."

"And who," she sniffled, "will be protecting me from you?"

There was a long pause. He stepped back from her. No more than a foot, perhaps, but she felt as if it were ten miles. She shuddered, and buried her face in her hands.

"There is that, isn't there?" he said bleakly. He leaned one hand on the immaculate polish of the car's hood and stared at her, perplexed. Finally he shrugged, climbed back into the car, spent another moment watching her through the windshield, and then drove away without saying another word.

Lucy arrived at the bank's doors just at nine o'clock. A guard unlocked the premises and she rushed in. Mr. Ledderman was talking to one of the other bank officers. When he spotted her he hurried her over to his desk.

"Well, what a delightful way to start the day off," he announced as he handed her into the chair next to his desk.

Lucy worked up a nice smile in return. He *was* such a nice person, her Mr. Ledderman, but she couldn't help a slight dig. "Does your fiancée know that you go around talking like that, Mr. Ledderman?"

"Know?" He gave her one of those dry giggles. "She encourages it, my dear. Funny you should say that. She and I have received a joint offer from a city out in Arizona. Sunshine, fresh air, and all that good stuff. And what can I do for you, Miss Borden?"

"Is it possible, Mr. Ledderman—another small loan?"

"Why, of course it's possible. In fact, it would be record setting."

"Oh?"

"Oh, yes. I have been with the bank for two years now, and this would be my last loan negotiation. Now, how much would you require? And shall we still consider it a mortgage extension?"

"Why—I guess. If that's the way it's done," small-voiced Lucy said. And she told him the amount she wanted. Not much, of course. Just enough, according to *her* calculations, to make four months' payments on her outstanding debt. And after that? *God will provide*, Angie Moore had said when they'd talked it over. But Angie was not a churchgoer, and Lucy was not exactly sure whether God paid attention to whatever sort of Christian the old lady was.

"Hardly a drop in the bucket," Mr. Ledderman said. "And, since the loan committee is all sitting around watching us, we'll push the papers through, shall we?"

Hardly an invitation to be avoided, Lucy told herself as she signed in three different places, then followed Ledderman around the bank while he presented the request to the board members, and each of them signed. And then, like the fatherly gentleman he was, he escorted her to the door and made his sad goodbyes.

It was too much for Lucy the sentimentalist. As he held the door open she threw her arms around his neck and gave him a heartfelt kiss.

"Well! At my own front door," Jim Proctor said from the back of her. "And with my own chief loan officer! Damn it, no wonder a man never has a chance in this town!" There was a touch of bitterness in his tone.

Ledderman, who had squeezed her enthusiastically, smiled. "Former chief," he said. "Just completing my last act, Mr. Proctor. I've finished up all my work, and was just escorting Lucastra out before I cashed in my accounts and made off."

"Lucastra? To Arizona?" Proctor asked.

"Sunshine. Fresh air," Lucy added.

Proctor looked at her with a wary look. "And you're going with him?"

"No, not me," Lucy replied. "He already has a girl of his own, you know. Mary Norris, the nurse."

"Ah. Yes of course, the nurse." There was a look of considerable relief around the corners of Jim Proctor's mouth. He obviously had no idea who Mary Norris was, but just the fact that she existed had certainly relieved his mind. "Yes. Wish you well. Goodbye, Ledderman." And he offered his hand.

Ledderman wore that crinkly little smile of his as he shook Proctor's hand. And offered Lucy one more little kiss on the tip of her nose.

"You'd better get at your accounts," Proctor said gruffly.

"Yes, of course. Oh, before I forget, how is our Miss Moore?"

"Improving," Lucy remarked. "Distinctly improving."

"Oh? That's—too bad," the loan officer commented as he walked back to his desk.

"And what do you suppose he means by that?" Jim Proctor mused.

"I don't know. He says something like that every time we meet."

"It makes no difference. Look, Lucy, I was some sort of a fool out there on the street this morning. I hope you might—well, Maude and I plan to go out boating this afternoon. Would you care to come with us, just for the—fresh air and all?"

"I'd really love to," Lucy admitted. "But I can't leave Angie all by herself, you know."

"I'll send one of my people over to spend the afternoon with her," he offered. "Would that do?"

"Only if it's somebody that Angie likes," Lucy said. "It can't just be anyone."

"My housekeeper," he offered. "She's a fine lady, and I believe she knows your—whatever your relationship is with Miss Moore."

"Just friends, good friends. We're no relation at all, to tell the truth, but Angie was a friend of my grandmother's and I've always kept up the connection."

He tucked her arm under his and towed her down to his office. "You're some kind of wonderful," he muttered as he seated her in one of the massive swinging chairs. The rest was indistinguishable. But, Lucy told herself, it was something like, "They don't make saints these days, do they?"

"I won't be but a few minutes," he added. "Wait for me?"

Why not? Lucy's heart said. She herself could barely manage a solemn nod of the head. After all, she told herself, it's quite a change, being considered a saint, after all those years of being known as a hellion!

Outside his door, where his secretary sat, she heard Jim Proctor say, "Find out where Mary Norris is. She's the nurse that goes around with Mr. Ledderman. Send her four dozen roses. The card? Just say, 'Thank heavens for you.'"

Lucy, knowing all the profits and punishments of eavesdropping, froze, her hands glued to the arms of the chair and holding on for dear life. And stopped breathing, to keep him from noticing her.

Life, she assured herself, was becoming more exciting all the time! Was this what they meant about falling in love? But he was such an impertinent man—such a steamroller—that she had to keep it to herself or he'd roll over her and leave her just a wet place in the middle of the road! Walk cautiously, Lucastra Borden!

"What the devil is going on here?" Jim Proctor slowed the Cadillac almost to a stop. There were more cars in front of the door of the Borden house than she had seen in weeks. But she knew no more about the crowd than Jim did.

"I don't know." Lucy was trying to be as meek and mild as possible, a disguise that was hard to maintain. And then she had a quick thought. "Maybe something's happened to Angie," she blurted out.

The brakes on the big car squealed. Lucy was out of the door before the wheels had stopped turning. All the noise, and there was a considerable amount, was coming from the back of the house. The front door was locked. Lucy fumbled for her key, and managed to get the door open.

Nothing was wrong with Angie Moore. She was sitting in her wheelchair, parked next to the open rear door, her back toward the front of the house, and there was an occasional chuckle from her ancient bones. Lucy skidded up to her chair. The old lady turned around, surprised.

"You're okay?" Lucy asked anxiously.

"Never been better," Angie returned, gesturing out of the door. "I haven't had this much fun since my father took me on that last cruise of the Old Fall River steamship line!"

"Then Maude?"

"Doing wonders," Angie retorted. "Go look."

Lucy looked, but behind her. In her newly cautious state of mind she hardly meant to plunge into battle without Jim. He was standing a few feet away, looking out of one of the windows. He awarded her a small smile, which launched Lucy into battle.

She took a deep breath, then stalked out onto the incomplete back porch, ready to fight dragons. Instead she found parents. A gaggle of people were milling around at the foot of the stairs, unable to get up on the porch because the builder had not yet finished things. Maude stood at the top of the stairs, hands on hips, a defiant gleam in her eye. It dissolved into a tear of thanks as she saw Lucy come up beside her.

"They're mad," the little girl said. "Absolutely mad!"

"You'd better believe it," the big man in the forefront of the crowd yelled. "We had a whole month of vacation planned, and now you dump my two stepdaughters back on me. I'm going to raise a little hell about this, lady!"

"And I want my money back," the woman behind him yelled. "With damages. I'll see you in court, Mrs. Borden!"

Lucy moved to the front rail. Things became unusually quiet. A little fantasy ran through Lucy's mind: I'm seven feet tall, and loaded with muscles, and they're just talkers, not fighters! She was quickly disillusioned. An arm came around her waist, and when she leaned back just an inch she found that her head was on his shoulder. Jim Proctor, of course. And with that, Lucy told herself, nobody can hurt me! So she leaned back another half inch and rested again, using his whole body to do so.

"I'm sorry you're inconvenienced," she told them all. "But I either had to close the school or go to jail!" A murmur of protest ran through the crowd. And now, Lucy told herself, is time for some creative magic. What my grandmother would have called Yankee lies. "And my fiancé said I was not to go to jail." Another murmur from the crowd. "Since I always do what he tells me, I closed the school." A silence from the crowd. Jim Proctor moved closer to her ear.

"What a darn liar," he whispered, and then took over the crowd.

Lucy listened, but hardly heard a word. He seemed to have started off with the preamble to the constitution, switched somewhere to the canticles of Job, put a little emphasis on the history of New England, and then summarized with some veiled threats about how awful it would be for any of them to get on the wrong side of the town's premier banker. They all seemed to agree, and drifted away by twos and threes.

Lucy watched them, her mouth half open in surprise. He chuckled in her ear. "And that's how it's done, my dear fiancée."

Lucy gathered up all her strength and turned to face him. "I am *not* your dear fiancée," she muttered at the second button of his shirt. "That was really a subterfuge." Her eyes went upward one button, to where his chin towered over her head. "Everybody is entitled to a subterfuge. And we are *not* going to be married."

"Stamp your foot," he advised. "It sounds much more firm when you do that."

"Mr. Proctor." She drew herself up to her fullest, and glared at him. A diversion is required, she told herself. And might have said something else in the same vein, when she remembered what Angie had said that morning. A sackful of papers. And who better to help her wade through them than——?

"Mr. Proctor. Jim," she said in her sweetest tones. "I forgot something. I can't go sailing with you. Angie and I—we have a problem."

"I got a problem too," Maude interrupted. "And mine is more important. Are you gonna marry my father?"

"Maude!"

"Well, Daddy, it's the most importantest thing in the world for me. Are you gonna marry my dad?"

"I—haven't thought it over well enough," Lucy stammered. "It's a very important step, getting married and all, and your father——"

"Is not the sweetest man in the world," Jim interrupted. "Now you just let Lucy make up her own mind. We wouldn't want her to marry me because we pressured her to do so, would we?"

"We sure would," Maude muttered. "Any ways possible. You don't have this big problem. You can go around the town with all kinds of women, but me, I need a mother!"

"What's this about him going around the town with all kinds of women?" Lucy inquired.

"Let's take a look at your *other* problem first, Lucy," Jim said hastily. "The walls have ears. Maude, you run up to the house and see if Mrs. Winters can whip up a fancy meal for all of us. Something portable. The men can carry it down and we'll all eat here at Lucy's house."

"But——"

"Go!"

"Nobody pays me no attention," the child muttered. "Lucy?" She seemed to jump across the space between them, just barely close enough for Lucy to catch her. Maude hugged her with all her strength, almost knocking the pair of them over. "I love you," she murmured in Lucy's ear.

"And I love you too," that one returned.

"Tomorrow. We go sailing tomorrow," Jim said wearily.

"It's only ten-thirty," Lucy told him. "Just the shank of the night."

"Yeah," he said, sighing. "Is there anything else in the bag?"

"Not in this one."

"You mean to tell me there's another bag?" Jim looked at the dining-room table, extended to its fullest, and stacked knee-high with little piles of papers, some so old that they crackled when moved.

"Just one. Why don't we stop and take a break?"

"Good idea. Look at this pile. I haven't seen any Northern Pacific preferred bonds outside of a museum. And I don't honestly know whether they have any value or not."

"And this pile over here?"

"That's for real. Those are Federal bonds. Good at maturity and forever afterward, and she can surely cash the lot. For—good Lord—I haven't the slightest idea. No interest has been paid since Caesar was a pup. And this pile over here—I'm not sure, but I'd swear it was Confederate money! Where did you get all this, Angie?"

"I'm not sure. Those last piles seemed to come in thick and fast when both my uncles died in the same week. I expect Uncle Willie saved it all. He used to save everything from string to baseball cards." A moment's pause; the old lady was tired. Two hours past her bedtime, and tired—but happy. Now it needn't be a joke, the old lady thought; now I've got something to leave for Lucy if things don't work out right. "And I'm not going to make a single bet from this time onward," she promised. The others laughed at her, and Lucy helped her to bed.

When she came back out into the dining room Lucy stretched, arching her back, flexing her arms like a cat scratching at the new furniture.

"Backache?" he asked.

"From leaning over the table," she said. "And eyes too. I never realized how little light we have in this room. I'm glad we got a start on this. I can see Angie's feeling ever so much better. She's not been well lately. Perhaps it's too cramped here. It's a big house, but with a lot of very small rooms. I can't help worrying about her."

"You would," he said as he tugged her over to sit on his lap. "You have the conscience of the world in your hands, Lucastra Borden. All tucked up inside your tiny self."

"I'm not tiny," she returned, and blushed fiercely. But there was no force in the statement. Her life was fast becoming—placid? Like the cow chewing its cud in the meadow? Like the woman who had been caught up in the flood tide of love, and hardly cared where the stream would take her.

"No, of course you're not tiny," he agreed. In fact, he told himself, I'm so damn satisfied with the world that I'd agree to almost anything. If only I could be sure.

"What do you think we ought to do next?"

"Why, I think we ought to kiss each other half to death."

She banged against his shoulder with one fist. "Not about us. About her. About Angie."

"This is the sort of thing you ought to turn to a banker for solutions," he said. "I've got a clerk or two who could inventory and figure values, and things like that. But we also ought to get Angie a good lawyer to look after her."

"I like that when you say it . . . *we ought to*. Are we truly a *we*, Jim?"

"Really, truly. There's nothing to part us now, lovable Lucy."

"I wish you weren't laughing when you said that."

"I had my fingers crossed."

"I have to tell you, I don't know anything at all about marrying, and things like that. My mother died so long ago, and——"

"Just what I need." He chuckled again. "Everything I want you to know about marrying, I'll teach you."

"That's big of you, Jim, but I'd want to check out your teeth before the ceremony. I remember the story about Little Red Riding Hood. She took a wolf's word for it—and wolves are one or two steps nicer than bankers. Bankers are notorious."

"Why, Lucy Borden, you cut me to the quick. How do you figure that?"

"Well, the day after I met you you foreclosed on the Merit Nursing Home, and they had to take all those poor patients out into the street. Didn't you think that was particularly mean?"

"I think you must have me confused with some other banker," he said. "I certainly didn't foreclose on the home. It's possible that I *might* have if I held the mortgage, but I didn't.''

Lucy wiggled a little on his lap, giving him more sensations than he cared to show. "I'm thankful, then, that it wasn't you," she said. "But you would have?"

"Without a doubt. I don't own the bank, you understand. There are depositors and shareholders. I run the bank, and try to make a little money for myself and for the shareholders. It's the depositors' money I use to do that. So anyone who fools around with mortgages at *my* bank can expect to pay up on time, or else!''

It was hard for a woman to tell whether her man was speaking sincerely or not, especially when his hands were running up and down her back, and his eyes were almost slits of concentration. And when those fingers fumbled at her back and he said, in some agitation, "How in the world do you get this thing open?" that was when any self-respecting female *had* to understand that theirs was not to be a platonic relationship.

"There are little buttons down the front," she said, but then, when his hand moved in that direction, she jumped up off his lap, shook herself out, and moved around the other side of the table.

"So." He got up stiffly. Lucy could sympathize. She was not a lightweight girl, and had been sitting on his lap for over half an hour. "So," he repeated, "and that's the end of today's dalliance?"

"You'd better believe it."

"Nothing doing until after the wedding?"

"Oh, Lord, Jim," she said as she fled into his arms. "I don't know what's come over me. I think I'm falling in love with you, and I don't even *like* you."

"We could always spend the night together, and see what comes up," he offered. "No pun intended."

"Thank you for the offer," she replied firmly. "My bedroom door opens up just past the altar. That's what my grandmother always told me, and I believe it. You'd better go home and get some sleep. Maude will be sleep-walking again."

"Not a chance," he said. "Not a step or whimper out of her since we sent her sweet Aunt Eloise away. Oh, I can see you're a tough cookie, Lucastra Borden."

"And I sleep with my eyes open," she warned him. "Good night, Mr. Proctor."

He was laughing when he walked out of the door. Lucy closed it behind him, and then leaned against it, dreaming of her heart's sweet prize. "Anyone who fools around with mortgages at *my* bank can expect to pay up on time, or else!" In a second her sweet dream turned to nightmare. Who else in town was trying her best not to pay off her mortgage? Who else but Lucastra Borden? And when he found out? Great gobs of golden goose grease!

Which explained why she was shivering and shaking as she made her way upstairs to bed. She paused for a moment in the upstairs hall, looking out of the window toward the road. Someone was out there in the darkness, under the maple tree just across the street. He wasn't much of a watchman; he lit a cigarette, and gave his position away. Lucy could instantly feel her stomach settle as she watched. Jim's guard, she told herself, and managed to stop shaking. He's watching over us, no matter what! And it's just like him not to tell. Maybe I do love him?

CHAPTER SEVEN

LUCY came downstairs the next day, all smiles and happiness, only to find that the weather was out to get her. Fog was rolling in from the Atlantic. Heavy gray masses of wet fog. It was possible to see all the way across Mattapoisett harbor, but just barely. The buildings over there on Mattapoisett Neck were completely blanked out. "Darn!" she exclaimed as she came in off the back porch. "We were going sailing today!"

"Don't get down in the mouth," Angie coaxed. "You can sail around the harbor, you know, you don't have to go out into the ocean. What's for breakfast?"

"Would you believe, potato pancakes?"

"I think I've gained five pounds since I came home—I mean, since I left the——"

"You were right the first time." Lucy came up behind Angie and hugged her gently. "Since you came home."

"You know just what to say," Angie murmured. "But just suppose——"

"Just suppose what?"

"Just suppose, in a fit of madness, say, you decide to marry that bank feller. Then what?"

"Then nothing," Lucy said, adding another possessive hug. "Things go on as usual. I haven't told him yet, but—if we do marry he'll have to take us *all* on." And then a hurried denial. "Of course, you know there's really nothing firm about marrying."

"He doesn't think that way. All you have to do is watch his eyes, girl, when he's looking at you. Lord, isn't that something? By the time you get old enough to know what men are thinking you're too old to do anything about it! Now, how about some scrambled eggs on the side?"

The two of them were hard at it when a hail came from outside, footsteps went around the house, and Maude and her father tumbled in through the front door. The little girl was dressed in a bright yellow one-piece bathing suit, with her hair up in loose braids. Her father seemed to be dressed casually, but as he came into the light Lucy noted that his casual clothes were obviously of the best. White trousers, a blue pullover, and a pair of deck shoes were on his feet.

It doesn't take much to put me in the shade, Lucy told herself as she looked down at her own shabby jeans. This guy is going to give me a permanent inferiority complex!

"I forgot entirely that you don't have your back steps in service," Jim Proctor said. "Good morning, beauty." With which he kissed Angie, and then hesitated for the barest moment. "And you too, Lucy." A gentle kiss. It was pleasant. Lucy turned bright red and backed away.

Maude was more enthusiastic. She ran at Lucy, jumped the last few feet, and almost knocked them both to the ground. "We're going fishing. You and me and Dad!"

"Oh, are we? But Angie and I have to finish our breakfast and——"

"I'll help you."

"Maude!" He shrugged. "You wouldn't know she's just gotten up from the table. And Mrs. Winters will be down in a few minutes. She's going to spend the morning with you, Angie."

"I want to thank you, but it really wasn't necessary, was it?" Lucy said as she began to clear the table.

"Thank me? For what?"

"For the guards last night. It gives a girl a certain sense of security, you know." She turned to offer him another hug, which he accepted.

"Come on, now, here comes Mrs. Winters. Will everything be okay, Angie?"

"Everything," the old lady commented. "You all have a good time, and keep off the rocks. Do either of you have a fishing license?"

"No," he said, laughing. "But then neither one of us has any bait, either."

His boat was a Seasled, a fourteen-foot fiberglass catboat, matronly wide and relatively shallow draft with a centerboard. It was moored some ten feet off the little jetty in front of his house. The tide was high. Not a breath of wind stirred the slowly lapping waves. "We gotta swim?" Maude asked.

"Yes," her father said. "Unless you would rather use the rubber dinghy down there? Scoot down and check it out."

As the child ran gleefully ahead of them Lucy took the moment to set things straight. "Just what is the purpose of this expedition, Mr. Proctor?"

"It's called dating," he said, and then grinned at her. "Of course, it's not usual to take my daughter along with me, but I thought we might give it a try. You are being courted, Miss Borden."

"Am I really?" Lucy nibbled on her lower lip, and then grinned back at him. "Courting? Well, I'll reserve judgment for the moment."

He didn't look too happy. "Come on," he said, and started for the dinghy. Lucy trailed along behind, thinking.

The little rubber boat was well-stocked with picnic baskets, leaving hardly enough room for three people. But with a little judicious squirming and yelling and pushing they finally made it out to the anchorage.

The single gaff-rigged sail went up easily. It was almost bigger than the boat. It gathered in what little wind there was, and the little craft began to glide southeastward, following the shoreline past Ned's Point light, and then turning east, coasting parallel to Pico Beach and Crescent Beach, and then curving gently southward until Strawberry Point was just off their lee. He dropped anchor there and doused the sail. With such light winds, it had taken them an hour to cover the small distance.

"Now," he said, "we fish." Lucy was snugged down in the stern of the open cockpit, one arm resting on the combing, the other hand on the tiller. Jim plumped himself down next to her, so closely penned in between tiller and combing that there was no room to wiggle. Which, Lucy thought, is no bad thing! When his arm came around her shoulders it seemed pleasantly simple.

"No poles," Lucy pointed out.

"Maude has hers," he said. "Up in the bow. You and I, we watch."

There was no doubt that the little girl knew just what to do. In another minute she was straddling the bow, her pole in hand, and line in the water.

"And all we do is watch?" she murmured.

"That—and anything else that comes to mind," he drawled.

"Does anybody ever catch fish in this area?" Somehow she found it impossible to keep her voice in its normal low register. Each word was coming out in a gasp. His hand, the one stretched over her shoulder, was descending perilously close to her breast.

"Not that I ever heard of," he answered. "It doesn't matter. Maude doesn't care, and we've got other fish to fry."

That hand came down another half inch, and was riding the top of her breast, separated from her skin by only the thickness of her thin cotton dress.

Lucy jumped nervously. *Other fish to fry*? "I—I'm hungry," she prattled. "If there's a sandwich in the basket I'd——"

"Lord, I'd forgotten," he said, sighing. "Are you sure you're not descended from the Puritan settlers?"

"Oh, but I am," she said hurriedly. "And the Pilgrims too, and——"

"Daddy?" Maude sounded somewhat concerned. He looked up at her.

"Daddy, the town just disappeared."

He looked back. The fog had ghosted across the harbor, and shut out everything in sight. At the same time something in his pocket began to beep at him. He pulled the little plastic box out, and consulted. "Hey, I'm sorry," he told them both, "but someone at the bank wants me. We'd better get back home as quick as we can."

"You're lucky you've got a beeper to distract us," Lucy whispered in his ear.

"Why, Lucy," somehow he made it sound so casual, "you distrust me?"

"Not me," she giggled. "But I would guess that if we don't get ashore in the next half hour we'll be out here all night!"

"Never try to con a Yankee, huh?" He pulled himself up, managed to get the anchor on board in record time, and slotted the sail back up. The boat heeled slightly, began to chuckle as it cut the rising waves, and headed straight for Ned's Point. Behind them, at the entrance to Cape Cod, the massive foghorn on Cleveland Ledge was bellowing.

"Well, this is cozy," Lucy commented as she stretched out and relaxed. "All we have to do is——"

"Pray," Maude commented. The little girl was being serious in a difficult situation. The wind that had momentarily filled the sail blew itself out, and the massive canvas swung limply back and forth. The boat coasted to a stop.

"I'm not sure, but I think we're losing this race," Lucy said. "What do we do next, Captain?"

"Very simple," he said. He ducked his head down under the swinging boom and came up with a pair of large sticks.

"Oh, no," Lucy groaned.

"Something wrong? They are only oars, girl."

"Don't *only oars* me," she snapped at him. "Six years ago I had a date with Hoagy Smith, and we ran out of gas out by Angelico Point in a fog. I remember it well. It took us four hours to row back into the harbor."

"And what happened to him?" Maude asked.

"I don't know. I never ever saw him again!"

"I'm glad you're familiar with the instruments," Jim Proctor said. "Now, Lucy, you take the port side, and I'll take the starboard, and Maude, you take the tiller. Right?"

"Right," Lucy said smartly. "How far do we have to row, and who's going to know where to steer?"

"It's only about a mile to Ned's Point," he answered. "That shouldn't take long, should it? This is a lightweight fiberglass boat. And I'll give the directions. Lord, I know every rock and shoal in the area."

"I'll bet you do," Lucy commented sullenly. But she pushed the long oar out through the rowlock and tested her muscles. Even before the boat began to move her muscles ached.

He required a moment to give Maude her instructions. There was a small compass set in the combing. "We don't want to just row around in circles," he instructed. And then he came forward and took up his own oar.

Light as the craft was, it took a few strokes to get it moving. And at every stroke forward the face of the fog bank was creeping up on them. Eventually it enveloped them, leaving them at the center of a fifty-foot world.

"Daddy, I don't like this," Maude whined.

"Not to worry," the sweating banker said. "I know every shoal and rock in this neighborhood." There was a thump at just that moment, and the centerboard bounced up in its well, then fell back down again. The boat stutter-stepped, gathered up strength again, and moved forward. "See?" he said. "There's one of them now."

"*Funnee*," his daughter commented as he took a tighter grip on the staff of the tiller. "Lucy? Do something!"

"I'm doing something." Lucy was almost out of breath, and the bump had killed their headway. She leaned into her oar, trying to synchronize her movements with his. It was difficult. He had thrown off his shirt and stood to his oar like some Viking. He didn't look like a banker; his muscles flexed like cables. He rowed as if he might be out in the pond at the park, where there was not a speck of fog to contaminate his movement.

"Daydreaming?" Lucy jumped. She had been laying on her oar while watching him, her mind a million miles away.

"Just—watching to see how it's done," she mumbled. "Are we going in the right direction, Maude?"

"I dunno," the child responded. "All the directions look the same."

"Just watch the compass!" her father said. It was the first time that Lucy had ever heard him shout at his child. She was so startled that she stopped rowing again and looked at him.

"Don't stare at me," he shouted. "Row! Row now."

"I'm rowing," she muttered under her breath. And put all the muscle she had to offer in the moving. But her mind was busy. Simon Legree, she muttered. Roman slaves. Tote that barr'l, lift that bale. Row. Thank heavens he doesn't have a whip!

They had been rowing for about an hour when Maude said again, "I'm scared." The child was almost crying.

"Everything's in good hands," Lucy said without believing it. "Your father has everything under control." The little head dropped back on the combing as Maude stifled a sob.

"I'm scared," the child repeated. "I'm gonna be the only girl in the third grade to be lost at sea and *drowneded*."

"Nonsense," Lucy said. "We're in the middle of an almost completely enclosed harbor. There are hundreds of people all around us, doing common ordinary things. And your dad knows everything. We have to trust in his judgment and sailing skills." She fumbled around at her feet, where one of the baskets was located. In it, she remembered, she had placed her light sweater. Now, with a considerable amount of squirming, she retrieved it, and tossed it back to where the child sat shivering. "There. Better?"

"Better. Tell me I ain't scared."

"You're not scared, child. There's nothing to be scared about."

"Not a thing," her father commented. "But it would be a lot easier if you would not stop rowing, woman! Everything is under control. I know just where we are, and——" God, or perhaps one of the archangels, interrupted. The little catboat, barely coasting along, bounced off another rock. The centerboard chattered up and down.

"There's a light," Maude shouted excitedly. "I can see a light!" Jim turned to look forward over his shoulder. There was indeed a light, directly in front of them, a very big light.

"Hey," he said, laughing. "We've got it made, we've——" And at that very moment the catboat bumped over another rock and slid up on to a tiny spit of sand, driving hard enough to beach itself. The sudden stop dashed them all forward in a temporary huddle, from which he made an instant recovery.

"Are you all right, Maude?"

"I bumped my arm," she returned.

"And you, Lucy?" And isn't that the proper order of priority? she told herself. Check on his daughter first. Am I jealous? Perhaps a little bit. He's got things in the right order for sure.

"I'm all right," she reported. "Battered and bruised and all right."

"Good girl." He patted her not too gently on her posterior, and then moved to cast off the sheets and loosen the lines that held the sail and boom. All three of them ducked as the boom swayed back and forth for a moment, and then settled at an angle across the cockpit. He lashed it down.

Jim Proctor managed to catch his breath as he slumped back in the cockpit. "See," he said weakly. "There we are."

"There we are where?" His daughter insisted on knowing, and would not give up. The wind picked up, tearing holes in the fog bank. The boat was driven another few inches up on the sand, firmly and safely aground.

"Why—right where I expected," Jim said. Directly in front of them was the small tower of Ned's Point lighthouse, its beam hard at work. "Right at Ned's Point. Everybody out!"

Not everyone who lived by the sea was a sailor. Not every woman, adrift on the ocean of love, was possessed of the inner strength to dull her own fears as she comforted another. Lucy was one of those. Confidence oozed out of her. Maude, feeling the comfort, squeezed herself back into Lucy's arms. "I wasn't scared," she muttered.

"Me neither," Lucy assured her. "After all, we had your father to look after us."

"Spare me all the praise," Jim Proctor said as he gathered them both up in his arms. "At least I'm willing to admit it. I was scared——"

"Jim!"

"I—was concerned," he amended. "C'mon, this is the end of the line. From here on we walk!"

He grinned at the collective moan, and then urged them both out on the sand, passing the baskets up to them. Ned's Point was actually a small park, in the center of which stood the light that had, for years, marked the entrance to the harbor. A couple of benches provided places, in better weather, where people might sit and watch the ocean. The trio struggled up the slight incline, appropriated one of the benches, and collapsed.

"Well," all three of them said in unison, and then laughed at each other.

"I was sure we'd be okay," Maude said brightly. "My dad can do anything."

"Have a sandwich and shut up," her dad told her as he reached into the picnic basket.

"Your daughter's absolutely right," Lucy chimed in. And for the first time in her young life she felt it to be true. Not since her father had died had Lucy felt the comfort of leaning on someone stronger than herself. But he's not *my* father figure, she muttered as she received the next soggy tuna-fish sandwich. He's—he's my knight in shining armor? Of course, it was a stupid thing to go sailing on a foggy day. But he overcame that bad decision, called on his experience to bring them back to safe harbor—and...no man is perfect, but Jim Proctor is as close to it as a girl like me requires. Maybe it's not true that I don't like him! *N'est-ce pas?*

The tuna-fish sandwich tasted about as bad as any salt-soaked food could be. Maude started to complain, looked up at her father, and squashed the comment. He was beginning to look like someone just down from Mount Ararat. Without thinking, Lucy looked for the stone tablets under his arm. He gnawed on his food, and looked around. The beeper in his pocket sounded off again. He shook his head. "I took up banking because you never had to work on the weekends," he said wryly. "And now look at me. Saturday noon, and already they're trying to get me."

It was ridiculous. The fog still shrouded their world. Beyond the fifty-foot circle which contained them and the lighthouse, everything was a gray maze. And still his beeper shrilled, summoning him back to the world of Cadillacs and counting houses.

"Well, all we have to do is walk down the road here," pragmatic Lucastra announced. "It can hardly be more than a half mile to our front door. We'll leave the baskets——"

"And the boat," Jim Proctor interrupted.

"That's littering," Maude contributed.

"But we'll send someone back up here to pick things up——"

"After the fog lifts," Lucy announced firmly. "Up, up and away."

"I wish you was Superman," Maude said moments later. "Then you could fly us——"

"Don't push your luck," her father chided. "Walk, now."

Maude danced in front of them as they walked down the narrow road. Lucy tucked her arm in Jim's. "What's this all about?" she asked softly, so that the child could not hear.

"All about?" he asked. "The fog?"

"Not the fog, silly. The day. Why?"

"Oh, that." He laid his hand over hers as they slowed. "As I said, it's an old-fashioned thing called *a date*. Surely a good-looking woman like you has been out on dates before?"

"Well—yes, I have. But never with somebody who took me out into the fog and——"

"So perhaps I'm not very good at it," he interrupted, irritated. "I've spent a lot of time trying to make money. My first wife was sort of gift-wrapped and mailed to me."

"With the fog and all, I think you've done very well," she told him. "Especially with your daughter along. That's a first for me, dating with a man and his daughter. And it's been very nice. Maybe we could do it again some time?" She squeezed his arm. His irritation disappeared as they walked contentedly behind Maude. Maybe we could, Lucy told herself. The wet dripping of the fog no longer bothered her. The three of them were walking together, sharing a circular world of no more than fifty feet in diameter, and it was all she needed.

They had gone about a quarter of the distance home when an old Pontiac came cruising up behind them at low speed. The driver stopped.

"Tough day to be going out any place," Jim Proctor offered as they all squeezed into the car.

"Ayup," the driver commented. He was strictly the old salt type, with a red face fringed by a white beard. "You folk got the right idea. Walk whenever you can. Wouldn't be goin' out at all, myself, if it wasn't for some idiot calling in an emergency radio signal from a power boat. I'm with the coast guard reserve. We answer all calls. I hope the jackass plotted his course correctly. Can you imagine? Running off into the fog bank with no Loran, or radar, or anything? And not enough gasoline to get home with?''

"No, I can't imagine," Jim Proctor said, shushing his daughter at the same time. "Here's our house. Thank you for the lift."

"You're a lucky man," Lucy whispered in his ear as he helped her out of the car. He glared at her, and hurried her along.

Both Angie and Mrs. Winters rushed to the door when they heard the footsteps and the car engine. "Well, thank the Lord," Angie said. "We were beginning to worry about you. Everything okay?"

"Everything's fine," Jim reported as he dashed for the telephone. "We had a little trouble, but I suppose everyone does on a day like this. Hello?"

"The man in the car was from the coast guard," Maude reported. "He said anybody who went out on a boat on a day like this ought to have his head examined."

"I think you'd better get upstairs and put on something warm," Lucy coaxed. "You left clothes here the last time you stayed over."

"Damn!" Jim Proctor, putting the telephone down. "I can't believe it."

"Believe what?" Angie asked.

"It's Saturday afternoon," Jim said disgustedly, "and a team of Federal examiners have arrived to spot-check the books. This is worse than——"

"I'll drive you down," Lucy volunteered.

"No need. I've called for my chauffeur to come. But I would appreciate it if Maude might stay until I get through with this nonsense. I'd forgotten that I gave my two guards the weekend off. I had thought that we——" The glint in his eye was very strong indeed. One of his hands stroked Lucy's shoulder, and had the tendency to slip even lower.

"That's the way it goes," she said as she hurriedly backed away from him. "Be careful. This fog is everywhere. I'll build up a fire to take the chill off. I think we have some hot dogs we could roast in the fireplace. Mrs. Winters? There's no need for you to stay if you can find a way to get into town."

"I'll take her with me," Jim said as he looked out of the window. "The car's here." There was a flurry of movement as the pair of them moved toward the door.

"But you're soaking wet, Jimbo," Angie protested. "Surely you can change clothes before going in to work?"

"Don't worry," he returned. "I'm mad enough now to dry these things off in a few minutes by sheer anger. Don't you all be concerned. Have a good day. And Lucy, it was a nice day—maybe we can do this again some time."

"Maybe we can." Lucy giggled, knowing how much more he wanted to do. And would I try terribly hard to stop him? she asked herself.

Maude came bounding down the stairs just as her father started out of the door. She was dressed in jeans and a white blouse, with her hair all askew.

"Daddy?" He paused. She ran across the floor and threw herself at him. He picked her up and held her high over his head before he kissed her. "I can't go with you?"

"Not this time, love. You're going to stay here with Lucy, and cook your lunch over a fire."

"I like that. Me and Lucy——"

"Lucy and I," Angie corrected.

"Yes, Lucy and I gotta get better acquainted, huh? Mrs. Winters, did you know that Lucy is gonna be my new mother?"

"Well—it's a little premature," Lucy protested. "We haven't——"

"Yes, we have," he interrupted. "Consider it as good as done. Next Tuesday morning, at the Congregational Church. Eleven o'clock." And with that he walked out and the door slammed behind him.

"Ooh!" Lucy gasped as she pounded both hands on the closed door. "That infuriating man! He takes everything he says as if it were cast in gold! And he never listens. I've told him *no* a dozen times! I'd love to pound him right square in the nose!"

"Then why don't you?" Angie asked softly.

"Because—I—I'm afraid he might hit me back." Lucy ducked her head to avoid the two pairs of questioning eyes. Having raved for what seemed like weeks about the quality of That Man, she could find no sure way to announce her change of mind. And one could hardly consider punching the man one loved right in the mouth. Could one?

"Ah," Angie said.

"I won't let him," Maude said sturdily. "Not even my dad. I need you to be my mother. If he raises a hand to you, Lucy, I'll—I'll bite his ankle!"

"And that," Lucy said, "is probably the best offer I've had in weeks. Shall we get at the lunch?"

CHAPTER EIGHT

"I'M SO darn stiff," Lucy said as she rolled over on the towel and let the sun get at her back.

"I'll just put on some of this sunscreen, and give you a massage as well," Jim offered, and started to work before she could raise an objection. His hands, covered with the cream, were soft and smooth. His fingers dug into the muscles around her neck. Lucy sighed with contentment.

"Not bad for a banker," she teased as she rolled over on her back.

"Don't say that," he returned. "I might not always be a banker. There are a million things I'd rather be."

"Are you two going to sit there on the blanket all day?" Maude came running by. Life, as ever, moved on a speedy track for little girls.

"We'll be along in a minute," Lucy called after her. The child ran for the water and dived in.

"Lord, what a way to conduct a courtship," he said, sighing.

"Oh? Is that what's going on today? I thought you had enough of that yesterday?"

"Not hardly, woman. And there isn't that much time left. We're getting married on Tuesday." Oh, is that so? Lucy thought. Why is it that I really don't believe it? Even if I might want to? *That* thought she was unable to reason.

It was just as well she needn't change the subject. He did it for her. One of his fingers slipped under the edge of her bathing suit. "And don't tell me it doesn't feel good," he murmured. There was a look of doubt on his face.

"I wouldn't object," she said brightly. "But your daughter's watching, and I think she's coming this way."

In the moment that hung between their thoughts the waves took over, singing their waltz on the beach. And the sea gulls, back again to hunt. Some of them almost domesticated, following boats in the harbor, waiting for someone to throw rubbish over the side. And still a few in the wild state, hunting shellfish, dropping them from a height on neighborhood rocks to break the shells, and then fighting their flock members for the contents. Lucy sighed. All this was home to her, the beach, the sea, the birds, the house— the man?

"Roll over," he commanded. Almost unconsciously she obeyed.

"Nice legs."

"Don't, please. Don't catalog me as if I were on sale or something."

His hands became busy, moving up and down her thighs, spreading the sun block.

"Have you heard from Eloise?" she asked drowsily.

"Just yesterday," he said. "Actually, from her mother. Eloise is in a depression, I am informed, and her mother is about to take her on a round-the-world cruise. She wanted to know—Grandmother, that is, wants to know if she could take Maude along with her."

"Oh, Lord—you didn't?"

"Nope. I told Grandma that I'd love to have Maude go with her, but the child has a bad case of chicken pox."

"Which is a disease Grandmother hasn't had?"

"Clever girl. Which is a disease Grandmother hasn't had." Lucy stared over her shoulder at all the cracks and crags in his somber face. All justice, no mercy, she told herself. Suppose I ended up in front of his firing squad? He'd pull the trigger without a moment's remorse!

Church bells sounded in the distance. "Ten o'clock," she mused, and then sat up. "Good Lord, I'm going to miss services again. That makes——"

"What a conscience you have." He pushed her gently back into the sand. "That makes how many times this year?"

"I can't say," she mumbled. "There have been a few. Well, to tell the truth, there's been a heck of a lot of them." She sat up again, brushing his hands away.

Regretting the doing, but answering the dictates of conscience. It's bad enough, she told herself, to be lying here on the beach of a Sunday morning, enjoying life, while some man runs his hands up and down my body. Right out in public, too, when I ought to be in church!

"You're too late now," he said, chuckling. "So why hurry? After yesterday we could use a quiet day. I'd offer to take you sailing, but when they recovered our boat they found that there's a hole in the bow."

Lucy managed to come to her feet and brushed herself off. He stood too, holding the bottle of lotion in his hand, and wearing a pained expression on his face. Impulsively Lucy stretched up into the air and kissed his cheek. "I'm changing my opinion about you," she said. "You're really getting to be a nice man."

"I'm glad you feel that way," he said. "The wedding is still set for Tuesday, you know."

"Well, I don't know that you're all *that* nice," she commented as she turned and ran for the ocean. He came after her, like an Aztec warrior pursuing his next sacrifice.

The Proctors ate lunch with Lucy and Angie. It was getting to be a habit, one that both the ladies enjoyed. About three o'clock, when Maude's eyelids needed props to keep them up, Jim made his excuses, and took her back up the beach. Angie and Lucy watched them from the back porch as he strode along, his daughter perched on his shoulders, like a mahout driving an elephant.

"You like him, don't you?" Lucy asked.

"Yes. A fine young man." A touch of pain ran over the old woman's face, and then disappeared. "Knew his family, you might recollect. They produced fine men, and finer women."

Lucy had caught the change of expression, and came over to the wheelchair and smoothed the thin white hair that was blowing in the wind. "You're not feeling well, are you?"

"Oh, I'm all right."

"Don't tell me that. I may be young and stupid, but I'm not blind. Come on, now, confess."

Her ancient hand came up and rested on Lucy's. I hadn't noticed, Lucy scolded herself. Her skin is like transparent parchment. She's withering away right in front of my eyes, and I hadn't noticed! A massive guilt feeling invaded her mind.

"People don't live forever," Angie said. "I'm so looking forward to Tuesday."

"Tuesday? Why Tuesday?"

"Because I listen and watch, love, and I know you're going to marry him on Tuesday."

"Lord, am I that obvious? *He* doesn't know that, despite all his big talk."

"Oh, you'll marry him, all right. And—live happily ever after. Isn't that how it goes? And you know something else?"

"No. What?"

"On Tuesday I shall be ninety-three years old."

"On Tuesday? I didn't know that! Ninety-three? Wow!"

"Wow indeed." The voice grew weaker. "I live just to see that day, Lucy. I want so much to see that day before I——"

"Hey, none of that sob-story stuff. I knew you were getting along, but I never did know your birthday. We shall have a celebration, shall we?"

"Yes." And the faltering voice broke. "Right after the wedding. Won't that be nice?"

"Yes. That will be nice. Tired, are you?"

"I am. It's strange. I gave up taking naps almost eighty-five years ago, but I surely would like to have one now." She patted Lucy's hand. "You're a good girl, Lucy. Such a nice creature. I hope he deserves you."

"Or vice versa. Come on, now, let's get you out of the wind."

"No, don't ever say that. I don't ever want to be shut off from the wind and the sea. In fact, when I die——"

"Good Lord, let's not talk about *that* subject. Nobody's going to die. We have years and years in front of us."

"Everybody dies, Lucy. Dying is as much a part of living as—— Dear Lord, girl. Don't cry all over me!"

"I'm not." Lucy managed to sniff back the tears.

"Oh, and Lucy, when I *do* go I want you to have everything." Lucy raised a hand in protest. "No, no, don't argue. There isn't any one else. I told my lawyer last week. The will is in my strongbox, in my closet. All my relatives are scattered to the wind, my dear. I have outgrown all my generation. And there's something I want you to do for me. I would like to be cremated, and have my ashes scattered over the harbor.''

"Well, that's enough of that talk." Lucy managed to pull herself together, and in moments the old woman was in her bed. Not more than ten minutes later she was asleep.

Look how pale she is, Lucy told herself as she sat down in the chair by Angie's bed. She's been keeping up with us for days, doing everything, sharing everything, but she's worn herself out! Should I call the doctor? Well, perhaps not yet. Tomorrow for sure!

This is tomorrow, and tomorrow is Monday, according to the Lord's schedule, Lucy thought. A bright and sunny Monday. Angie was still asleep when Lucy stretched mightily, then tiptoed up the stairs for a quick shower. She had maintained the vigil all through the night, sitting in that chair by Angie's bed. The old woman had tossed and turned all night, babbling in her dreams. Smiling, weeping, all in turn, reliving her life. But, throughout it all, holding Lucy's hand, and objecting when that hand was withdrawn. As dawn came Angie had stilled, lying flat on her back, breathing heavily, and releasing that grip on Lucy's hand.

The hot water was refreshing. It loosened Lucy's muscles, gave her a new grip on life. A temporary grip, but new. Today was a new day. She smiled as she ran her eye over her wardrobe. Today he would certainly—or perhaps *she* would certainly say something that might truly bind them together for life. It was an amazing thought. One that she had never in all her life thought before.

Something light to wear. Something happy. An A-line shift, cotton to gently caress her figure, gold to reflect her happiness. And a little heart-shaped butterfly embroidered at her breast. Briefs only beneath it, because, after all, it was now August, and August by the water was a month for broiling. Moccasins, because shoes would hardly do. She went back down the stairs and checked. Angie was still sleeping, breathing throatily, but sleeping. And the first thing to do was call the doctor.

"There isn't really anything I can do," Dr. Halpern commented. "Mrs. Moore is old. Most of her parts have run down. But if it will make you any happier, Lucy, I'll send the paramedic team around—oh, say about ten o'clock, and they can bring her in to the hospital for a checkup if it seems necessary." Which is about the best I can do, Lucy thought. No doctors made house calls these days, not in America the beautiful. If you were really sick it was the ambulance for you, and the hospital, where all of medical science was marshaled to diagnose and cure. And the costs would be sky high! So treatment came in an ambulance driven by a pair of well-trained paramedical people, who either would or would not take Angie away to the hospital.

So Lucy walked around the house on cat's feet, avoiding noises, checking occasionally on Angie, and made her own breakfast. In the kitchen nook there was a small table fit for two, with a window out on the world of water. Lucy squeezed into it and had her toast and coffee, and then, after some further thought, an egg on toast, as she watched the boats moving in and out of the harbor, sailing over the horizon to the Lord knew where.

At eight o'clock Maude appeared on the scene and was promptly hushed with an explanation. The child peeked around the door into Angie's room, then came back out to the kitchen nook and sat down.

"No breakfast?" Lucy offered a leftover piece of toast.

"No breakfast. He got up early and went to the bank." There was no need to say who *he* was. "Mrs. Winters called in sick or something. No, it was her niece who was sick. So Dad said, 'Why don't you go down and bother Lucy for a while?' And I said, 'That's a fine idea. She makes good breakfastes. Lots better than you do.' And he made as if he was goin' to throw me out the window, and I would like two eggs, please."

"Breakfastes?"

"Yeah, you know. Plural for one breakfast. Don't you know nothin'?"

"I guess I don't, love. Okay. Two eggs. Orange juice. Milk."

"Coffee," the child said and ducked her head, which was a dead giveaway.

"When was the last time your dad allowed you coffee with breakfast, young lady?"

"Not never. But I thought that you, bein' nicer than he is, would at least let me try it?"

So Lucy, agreeable to being "nicer than he is," produced everything required, including a sample thimbleful of coffee. As she worked she puzzled. This was to be a glorious day. Mother nature was providing the setting, but Angie's apparent illness was darkening the day. Maybe the old lady was only sleeping it off, of course. They had lived an exciting few days, this little nuclear family of theirs. She could just be more tired than usual. So today we'll take things easy, and see what happens. With her hands divorced from her brain, Lucastra Borden made all the breakfast preparations.

Every time she went across the kitchen Lucy included a detour by Angie's bed. Nothing had changed. And every time Maude thought to say something she was hushed with a finger across the mouth. So it was not surprising that, when Jim Proctor banged his way into the house, both Maude and Lucy hushed him.

"What the hell?" he muttered. His face was flushed with anger. "I need to talk to you, Miss Borden!" Obviously he wasn't about to be shushed, so Lucy took him by the arm and ushered him out of the front door, away from the house.

"Angie's still asleep," she explained. "Now, what's this all about?"

"You know damn well what this is all about," he snapped. "The bank examiners came by on the week-end just because they had too busy a schedule to do everything they had to. Another bank up in Taunton closed its doors on Friday. Went belly-up because of too much unsecured money invested in real-estate loans. The same disease that's affecting all of New England."

Lucy made a sort of understanding noise, although she didn't understand a thing.

"So they spot-checked some of our loans," he continued. His voice was getting more and more harsh. "So what do you think they found?"

And Lucy, who hadn't the slightest idea, shrugged her shoulders. Only to find him gripping those same shoulders with heavy hands. "No, of course you don't know what they found." He gave her a rattle or two that sent her head around in circles. She made a weak protest.

"Don't give me that," he almost shouted. "I'll tell you what they found. Forty-two thousand dollars in loans to Lucastra Borden, all without any collateral at all. All, according to our departed Mr. Ledderman, issued based on 'expectations.' Now just what the hell does that mean?" Another shake of her shoulders, meant to get her brain in action, Lucy thought. But it was having just the reverse effect.

"Forty-two thousand dollars?" she gasped. "Don't *do* that." She broke away from his punishing hands and rubbed her shoulders. "I didn't think it was that much, but after a while it didn't seem worth it to count how much it was, you know."

"No, I don't know, you little schemer. What the devil did you need the money for?"

"Why, to fix my house," she stammered. "The roof leaked."

"Forty-two thousand dollars to fix up this old flea trap?"

"I wish you wouldn't keep saying that."

"Saying what?"

"Saying forty-two thousand dollars," she maintained stubbornly. "You make it sound immoral for me to borrow—that much. It was all perfectly legal, and I wish you wouldn't yell at me like that because——"

"Because you hadn't any intention at all of repaying it, did you?" He had come down from roaring at her to an almost sibilant whisper that cut through her like a knife. Was this the man she was going to marry? she asked herself desperately. Was this the man who was going to cherish and love her all her life? Was this the man?

"Of course I was going to repay you," she snapped. "I've got the first monthly payment all ready, in the drawer of my sewing machine. What the devil do you think I am, Mr. Proctor? Some thief?''

"You've got the money? Where the—where did you get it?'' He was advancing on her step by step; she was backing away until she bumped into the maple tree beside the house. Her tired mind was running off in all directions at the same time. All she could remember was that she just had to get away from this raving maniac.

"It's easy,'' she cried at him. "I went to the bank and borrowed it. Isn't that what banks are for?''

"You what? You went back to my bank and borrowed more money to pay the loan? What sort of a con game are you running?''

"Please,'' she begged, close to tears.

"Please? You think you can get away with it with *please*?''

And that was the final straw. Lucy vividly remembered. Plenty of justice, but not an ounce of mercy. And now he was turning it all on her. She took a deep breath to settle herself.

"Look, if you think I've done something illegal, go down to the police station and have them arrest me. Do you really think I'd marry you tomorrow after all——?''

"Forget it,'' he said bleakly. "The wedding's off. Where's my daughter?''

"Eating my breakfast,'' she muttered, and then backed herself up against the tree for support. He stomped away without a backward look.

And that, Lucy told herself, is a beginning to a good day? He certainly has stomped all over me. But I'm not going to let him make me cry. I *won't* do that. If I don't have anything else left in all the world, I have the Borden pride. He will *not* make me cry. Nobody can make me cry! Nobody!

She moved away from the tree and sniffed back the incipient tears, then brushed down her dress of gold, her dress of happiness, and stalked back into the house. Maude had disappeared. "Bad luck to them both," she muttered, but knew she didn't mean it at all. There was a sound from Angie's bedroom, which diverted her thoughts as she ran across the kitchen to the sick room.

"Good morning." The old lady looked up at her, eyes sparkling, but cheeks as pale as paper. "I seem to be sleeping over."

"It's only nine o'clock," Lucy said. "And you need the rest. We'll get you up and breakfasted. I called the doctor because I was worried about you. He's going to send somebody over later this morning. Now, shall we be up?"

"I—I think I'd rather not," Angie Moore said. "I don't seem to have much control over my legs this morning. Perhaps I could have breakfast in bed?"

"Of course you may. What would you like?" As she listened and chronicled all the separate things said, Lucy was becoming more and more perturbed. There was no doubt that Angie had suffered some internal change that was still dragging on her. The old lady was functioning more on courage than comfort. She seemed unable to control her left arm.

"Tea," Angie said. "For some reason I feel like having a cup of tea. We always had that at home when I was a girl, you know. Papa loved it. Tea and toast. Or muffins? You don't happen to have any muffins on hand?"

"Of course I do. They'll be ready in a minute. And maybe a little wash? You wouldn't want those medical people to pop in on you when you're looking peaked, would you?"

"And my new nightgown," Angie replied. "I've never worn that yet. On top of everything in the second drawer of my bureau."

So, with a morning full of work, Lucy set to, and when the medical people appeared and rang the front doorbell Angie was ready to hold court for all.

At the door Lucy found something she had not expected. Instead of only a couple of paramedics, the team was accompanied by a nurse. "Nurse practitioner," the young lady introduced herself. "Mallory Small. I work in association with Dr. Halpern. May we see the patient?"

The team followed Lucy around and into Angie's bedroom. The patient welcomed them with a great deal of spirit, and endured the indignity of having them take vital signs of all types, and finally the nurse made her own examination, talking quietly to the patient as she did so. When they had finished their work the three of them asked to be excused, and went off to the kitchen to confer.

"Nice," Angie said. "That's what you should have done, Lucy. Become a nurse."

"Nurse practitioner," Lucy commented. "That's a certificate almost as high as a doctor. But—well, you know I thought about it when I was twelve years old. Only one day I was out in the kitchen with my father, doing something or other. I forget what. All of a sudden I cut my finger. I remember I stood in the middle of the floor staring at this little cut, and the blood dripping on the floor. And my dad said that it wasn't much of a cut. But the blood—when I saw the blood I fainted. And that's when I decided I didn't want to be in the medical profession!"

"Silly. Just one little cut?"

"Excuse me. Miss Borden, could you step out here for a moment?"

"Bad news, I'll bet." But Angie didn't seem to be too concerned. In fact, she managed to work up a grin.

"Probably the bill," Lucy joked as she went out to join the medical team.

The two men were packing their gear. The nurse said, "Sometimes we have to be brutal in this world, Miss Borden. I take it that the patient is near and dear?"

"You could say that, certainly. Well, dear, at least. All her relatives are gone. Angie is alone in the world.

But there's no need to sugarcoat anything. Give it to me."

"Well, before I came over I had a long conference with Dr. Halpern. All my tests have indicated that what he felt when I left the office is certainly confirmed. To be straightforward, Miss Borden, there is really nothing we can do for Mrs. Moore. All her functions are gradually wearing down. There are some medicines I can prescribe to make her rest more comfortably. It's possible that bed rest may bring her up to snuff. Or we can take her to the hospital and try to make some heroic gestures to keep her alive. On the other hand, just by putting her in the ambulance and driving twenty miles to the hospital might do her in immediately."

"You mean——?" The enormity of it all struck Lucy full in the face. But I won't cry, she told herself fiercely. I didn't cry over Jim, and I won't cry over Angie. I'll keep up my strength so that she won't feel worse, and save my crying for—later. "You mean she might die?"

"Any minute, any hour. All we can really do is make her comfortable. And the only question you have to answer is, shall we leave her here in her home, in her loving surroundings, or shall we take her to hospital, hoping that we might possibly do something better?"

"I—understand," Lucy said quietly. "And your best professional estimate? What chance does she have to do better in the hospital?"

"One chance in a thousand." The nurse hesitated for a moment. "I'm presuming that you could take care of her here. That you would want to look after her?"

"Yes, I would." Lucy shook her head in amazement. Earlier this morning she had been struck by a thunderbolt. And now a second one. In the short space of a few hours the hand of fate had thrown her life completely out of balance. What to do?

"Angie is afraid of hospitals," she said.

"Many elderly patients are."

"And I'm all she has left in this world."

"Yes. Then I would recommend we leave her here with you."

Lord, tell me what to do. Lucy offered a silent prayer. Tell me what to do. But the sun shone, the wind blew, the birds cawed, and nobody was there to lift the burden from her slight shoulders. And so she finally said, "Angie has said more than once that she wants no heroic efforts to save her life. She's the last woman in the world who would want to end up in hospital surrounded by machines that barely keep her alive. Yes. Leave her with me."

"A good solution. Now, if she suddenly turns for the worse, don't hesitate to call us again."

"I won't."

"Dr. Halpern sent some prescriptions over to the pharmacy. They'll deliver in a few minutes. All the instructions are on the labels." The nurse, who had seen many such cases, nodded sympathetically, and went out to join her team. Lucy, who had spent her life making only small decisions, walked slowly back to the sick room, dragging her feet after having made the biggest decision in her young life.

Angie was still sitting up in bed, a bright smile on her face. "The news is all bad?"

"I—Angie, I don't know what to say."

"Straight from the shoulder, Lucy, that's always been the best way."

"They'll take you to the hospital if you like, but——"

"But there's nothing much they can do? I knew it would be like that, love. No, I'd rather stay here, surrounded by the little things I love. Come on, child, cheer up. Now, if you could help me lie down again, I think I'd like to nap a little longer."

The work was quickly done. Lucy brought in another cup of tea to soothe, and had one for herself.

"This is nice," Angie said. "Do you remember——? No, of course you don't. When I was sixteen. Grandfather took us all—there were six of us then, you know. Grandfather took us all to New York for the weekend, and we stayed in the Ritz and saw all the museums, but my cousin Bob, who was twenty-one at the time, sneaked me out one night to see one of those naughty Broadway plays, and oh, I felt so sophisticated! And then..."

The voice, which had been growing weaker with the telling, ran out, and she fell asleep. Lucy barely managed to rescue the teacup. There seemed nothing more to be done but watch.

About an hour later someone knocked on the front door. Lucy, who had been sitting next to Angie's bed, holding her hand, jumped up in surprise. But her sleepy mind quickly switched back to reality. Her builder, Mr. Henderson, was at the front door.

He stood apologetically, hat in hand, a concerned expression on his broad face. "I hear tell in the town that the old lady doesn't feel well?"

"That's true. I—she's not well at all."

"So, I thought, why don't I take my crew over to Church Street, where we have another job, and leave you in quiet for a few days?"

"That's a wonderful idea." Lucy managed a weak smile. "You won't forget us, though?"

"Not on your life, little lady. I see them big shots just up the way is all movin' out."

"Oh?" Lucy stepped out the door onto the little front porch. It was all true. A moving truck was parked by the front door, and men were carrying furniture out. And that's the icing on the cake, Lucy told herself. The wedding's off, and now he's off. How could I possibly let things get this far? I could have held him in my heart as the original rotten man, and avoided all this heartache. But no, lovable Miss Borden has to go playing games with the big bad wolf, and now look who's burned to a crisp! I wonder—what's happened to Maude?

"Then I'll be going along," Henderson told her.

"I—thank you for all your trouble," she told him.

"No trouble at all. Oops. Looks as if the little girl is comin' visitin'." And with that the big gruff man waved a casual salute and went out to his truck, parked at the curb.

The little girl is coming? Lucy stepped all the way out onto the porch, fastening the door open in case Angie should call. It was true. Little Maude was coming down the street pell-mell, as if the devil himself were behind her.

"Lucy," the child yelled. Lucastra Borden went down to the bottom step and waited. The child zoomed around the rosebush at the front corner of the house, and skidded to a stop.

"Oh, Lucy," she wailed, and fled into the welcoming arms.

There were tears galore. Tears of anger, tears of frustration. "He says you're not going to be my mother!"

"I'm afraid not, love. We—your father and I—have come to a disagreement about many things, and we're not going to be married after all."

"It's not because of me? It's not something I done wrong?"

"No. That's not any part of it. I still love you. I still would like to have you as my daughter. But it's impossible. Your father would rather murder me than marry me, I'm afraid. There, now, child."

"But I *want* you to be my mother." The little arms came around Lucy's neck and clung for dear life. "I *want* you to be——"

Tears struggled in Lucy's eyes to match those of the child. But I'm not going to cry, she commanded herself. Not for Maude, not for Angie, and, most of all, not for him. I'm not going to cry!

"You have to understand, Maude, that it isn't just you and me. There are three of us to consider. Your father thinks that I'm a bad influence, I think. At least he thinks that I'm a——" She stopped short. Whatever else Jim Proctor thought her to be, thief and liar were the two prominent ideas.

"Your father's a good man, Maude. He loves you. He'll do whatever he can to make you happy. I'm terribly sorry that marrying me is not one of those things. We must learn to live with it. You and I both. Now, dry up those tears, and scoot on back home. I really—wouldn't like it if your father had to come for you. Be a brave girl. Some day we may meet again, and if we do we'll laugh at the memories. Off you go."

Maude relaxed her grip and took one step backward. The tears were flowing madly. "I don't think so." The child sobbed all the more. "I don't feel like being a brave girl, and I'll never laugh when I think of you, and my father is a—dictator—and I——" And she spun around and ran off around the house, back to the eternal sea for comfort, while Lucy bit at her lower lip until it bled, and just managed to dab at her eyes with a tiny handkerchief which she had found in her pocket. Up the hill she could see Jim Proctor come out of the house. Looking for his daughter, Lucy told herself. And I can't stand to look at him again, and I don't want to be here if he comes down!

So she rushed into the house, telling herself that Angie was stirring and needed attention. Which was not true.

CHAPTER NINE

LUCY shifted in her chair and massaged her hand and wrist. All afternoon, and on into the night, she had sat by Angie's bedside. The old woman perked up in the middle of the afternoon, and was full of chatter about her youth. There was only one oddity. In every scene she talked as if Lucy herself were part of the happening, although much of the action took place long before the girl's birth.

"You remember Memphis, Lucy? When was that? Just before the Great War, in 1917, wasn't it? When we both were seventeen, and Grandpa took us to see the jazz festival? Wasn't that something? And Peter was there!"

"Yes, I remember," Lucy said. "Peter?"

"Ah, Peter. A fine broth of a boy, Lucy. As handsome as the day is long. We were—interested in each other." A long pause followed, almost as if the old lady was remembering the details.

"What about Peter, Angie?"

"Peter? Peter. Oh, he went to France in 1918, you remember? He was at Château-Thierry and the Argonne. I remember—we went to France, Daddy and

I, to see, you know, later. After the War. Peter is still there, at Château-Thierry.''

"He never came back?"

"He's—waiting there for me."

"That'll be nice, Angie."

"Yes. Nice."

Lucy remembered how often Angie used that word. "That would be nice"—her favorite expression. And now, reaching back into the vague distortions of over seventy years, she had dredged up Peter, who would have been nice, but went off to war and still lay in the French heartland. A lost romance? She looked down at the frail creature on the bed. Angie Moore was smiling, as if the memory was sweet. Her face was pale parchment, and now her lips were turning blue and her breath was becoming more shallow.

Only her massive self-control kept Lucy from breaking down and crying. Something had to be done. Something! As quick as thought Lucy dropped the aged hand again and raced for the telephone.

"Hang on," the telephone operator told her. "They're coming."

Lucy dropped the telephone and hurried back to the bedside. All her guilty fears arose around her. And here was another one. Had she sent Angie to the hospital earlier, things might have been different. Another bad decision. But when she got back to the bedside Angie was awake and smiling feebly.

"Don't hurry so, girl. You'll wear out your shoes."

"It was the telephone," Lucy gasped. "You know how they bother me. And all for nothing."

"Nothing's for nothing, Lucy. Everything has a meaning. I'm sorry, child."

"Sorry? What do you have to be sorry about?"

"I'm sorry because your wedding's tomorrow, child, and I won't be there to see it all happen." The patient held up an admonitory hand. "Now don't tease at me about things like this. I know what's happening. I've loved you for many years, my dear. Many years. I've felt that you were my very own daughter, and I'm so pleased that you will have Jimbo to look after you. Jimbo—where's Jimbo?"

And I'll not tell her the truth about that either, Lucy told herself as she gritted her teeth and swallowed all her anguish. "He's away—on business. He'll come by as soon as he gets back."

"Tomorrow, then. Oh, of course. A hardworking boy. He'll be good for you, Lucastra."

Good for you, Lucastra. Good for you, Lucastra. The words echoed around the room. Echoed and pounded on her ears. Struck at her heart until it vibrated past bearing. Dear Jim. "Yes, of course," she said.

In the distance Lucy could hear the siren of an ambulance coming in their direction. She looked down at her wristwatch. Only fifteen minutes since she had called. They'll be on time. I know they'll be on time! And surely they will have developed a new cure? Surely they would.

And it was just that moment that Angie's eyes opened again, an excited look flashed across her pale face, and somehow she managed to sit up in the bed. Lucy grabbed at her, holding her by the shoulders. There was a gleam of sheer delight in Angie's eyes.

"Oh, Lucy," she half whispered, "remember when we all went to the Ritz and the music on the patio was so beautiful, and we could see all the stars? And oh, we danced the night away. Remember? Oh, the wonderful dancing!" Still smiling, she closed her eyes as Lucy laid her back on her pillow. Don't cry, Lucy commanded herself. Don't cry!

The front doorbell rang, and immediately opened. The same two paramedics rushed in, pushed Lucy aside, and began their measurements. But only for a moment. Both of them came to a halt, and began to remove their instruments.

"Oh, no!" Lucy cried as she forced herself between them and threw herself across the bed. "Oh, God, no!"

"I'm sorry, ma'am," the senior of the two told her, and then turned to his partner. "There's a phone out in the living room, Harry. Call in and tell them that the patient is DOA."

Tuesday, August eighteenth. Tuesday I'm going to be married, Lucy told herself. She was sitting on the remnants of her as yet unrepaired back porch, staring out at the empty beach. No, Tuesday I didn't get married. I'm never going to get married, and Angie is never going to share the rest of our lives in happiness. Neither am I.

She fingered her plain black dress and stifled the forming tear. I am *not* going to cry, she told herself. "I am not going to cry!" The sullen waves danced up to the beach in front of her, curtsied, and fell back into the ocean. There was no sun. Clouds covered the heavens from horizon to horizon. Everything was dull, dismal, still. Even the gulls were respecting her privacy.

A man came around the corner of the house. Lucy looked up expectantly. But it was not Jim. Of course not. This stranger came over to her side.

"Ma'am. I'm from the funeral home. It's time to go to the memorial service."

"Yes," she croaked. Her throat was sore, her bottom lip chewed to pieces. It was hard to think. It was *last* Tuesday that I was going to be married. Last Tuesday when Jim left me. Last Tuesday when Angie left me. Last Tuesday. "I'm ready."

He helped her up gently, as if she were a hundred years old, and steered her around the house. A black limousine waited at the kerb. Room for seven people. They ushered her in to sit by herself. Her escort saw to her seating, then climbed into the driver's seat.

Lucy huddled in one corner of the massive car, fighting to hold back the tears. It had been this way for a week. Everyone wanted a decision. Lucy, shall we do this—or that? This sort of funeral—or that? These announcements—or those? And Lucastra Borden could not make a decision. Her usually sharp mind had fallen off the track. All she knew was that she mustn't cry! So now there was a memorial service for Angie. At least she had agreed on that much. But surely the moment she walked into the church there would be a horde of people who wanted some other decision? And I must not cry, she told herself fiercely.

The car came to a stop, and the driver helped her out. There were a few people waiting at the church doors. Angie's few old friends, most of them with canes or walkers or wheelchairs. A few people attracted by the crowd. And a reporter. A man Lucy had always considered to be a kindly friend, now rated as an enemy. She ducked her head and forced her way into the church and down the aisle to the Borden family pew.

The organ thundered something or other. The minister said something or other. Lucy huddled in the corner of the pew. I must not cry, she told herself, and could not remember *why*. She trembled, unable to follow the service.

Someone came down the side aisle and stopped by the end of her pew. Out of the corner of her eye she registered the presence, and then shifted over farther in the pew. The man came in the pew beside her. A large hand fell on her arm. She felt the electric tremor of his touch, and looked up to see who it was. "Oh, my God, Jim! Oh, my God." Said in a whisper so as not to disturb the singing. Her ever so independent head wobbled for a moment on a slim neck, which was too weak to support it, and then toppled over and landed against his chest. One of his massive arms came around her shoulders, holding her gently in place. The warmth surrounded her. "Cry, Lucy," he said.

Lucy took a deep breath to settle herself, and then she cried. Cried up a storm to measure all the pains and tribulations, all the days of suffering, all the pains of memory. She was still crying when the brief service ended, and then she cried some more, until she had sobbed it all out, resting there on his solidly warm chest. And at last she was at peace with her world once again.

There was noise and confusion in her house when Lucy awoke. Hammering and talking and giggles, as if an invasion had taken over. Slowly memories came back. She stirred, only slightly. The big figure sitting in the chair beside her bed stirred as well, stood up and shook himself, and then sat down and took her hand. He was a larger-than-life figure, outlined by the sunlight streaming through the window.

"What?" she mumbled.

"Sleeping pills," he told her softly. His hand stroked hers. It was a pleasant feeling to one who had known little pleasantness in the past week. "Dr. Halpern gave you a shot yesterday, and now pills. You've been running on an empty tank, love."

"I—don't understand." But I like the sound of the words, she told herself. *Love*? She turned slightly in his direction. Her eyes focused unwillingly. "But you've gone away."

"Only temporarily. Can you see me, Lucy?"

"Yes. Somehow you're out of focus, but I can see you."

"And hear me clearly."

"Yes. Oh, yes."

His hand squeezed hers gently. "I love you, Lucy Borden."

And what, she asked herself, does a girl say to something like that? "That's nice"? That was what Angie would have said, and somehow she felt that Angie was here in the room with her. Well, it had worked for years for Angela Moore, why not for Lucastra Borden?

"That's nice," she mumbled.

A chuckle from high overhead. He had risen, picked up something, and used a hand to raise her head off the pillow. "That's enough for now," he said. "Now drink this."

Obedient as a small child, she drank. Some of the liquid missed her mouth and ran down her chin. He lowered her head back on to the pillow, then wiped her chin.

"Go to sleep, child." Lucy could almost hear Angie say the same thing. The sound came from a long distance away, hollow, as if said into a barrel. And before she could think of anything witty to say she was asleep again.

The next time she woke up the sun had disappeared. A tiny glow from a night lamp cast shadows across the room. Dark shadows. Lucy squirmed in bed. The shadows bothered her. There was another figure sitting in the chair by her bed. A little girl, whose legs were not long enough to reach the floor. Lucy tried to say the name, but her voice could not handle the effort. She tried again, and produced a squeak. Then, on the third attempt, "Maude?"

The little figure moved; hurled itself across the intervening space and fell on top of her. Only a tiny weight, a squirming, cherishing weight. "Oh, Lucy! They said you might not—you know who I am?"

"Of course I do, silly. You're Maude Somebody. I remember you well. You have a monster of a man for a father. I forget his name. Give us a kiss, darling."

"They said I wasn't to disturb you. No touchin', no nothin'."

"I love you, Maude Somebody."

"F'goodness' sakes. Maude Proctor, not Maude Somebody. I love you too, Lucy."

"Who is 'they'? What do *they* know? Give us a kiss."

Given and received. One very moist kiss, aimed for her forehead but landing instead on the tip of Lucy's nose. But satisfactory, none the less.

"I don't think my dad would like that." But obviously the child did. She cuddled up, straddling Lucy's figure, and offered another.

"I don't think it matters," Lucy returned wryly. "There's only you and me here, so we can kiss whenever we please. And if your dad doesn't like it——?"

"Yes? If he don't like it?"

"I'll do something terrible to him to teach him a lesson."

A caution. The child ceased to squirm, and moved over beside Lucy in the bed, instead of resting on top of her. She was all seriousness now, and paying strict attention.

"You'll punish him?" Asked in such a tone as if she thought they were about to assassinate the Pope.

"Yes, I'll punish him. I'll marry the man. And that's a life sentence. Gee, I'm hungry!"

The child took one quick indrawn breath, and then kissed her again.

"Thank you, I think," Lucy said to the departing back. Feet slammed down the stairs. Feet moving fast—maybe faster—than the little girl could handle. And her voice, shouting as she ran.

"Dad! Dad!"

"Hush, Maude, we mustn't disturb Lucy."

"She's awake. She's awake already. And she says——"

"She says what?"

"She says I could kiss her and I did and I said you wouldn't like that 'cause that would wake her up and she said it was none of your business 'cause you weren't there in the room and so I could kiss her again and I said I loved her and she said she loved me and she said if you wanted to complain she was gonna punish you by marrying you, and—— Dad?''

But dad was halfway up the stairs before Maude could get to the period at the end of the sentence.

He came into her room almost out of breath. She looked at him and liked what she saw. There's a difference, she told herself, but I don't know what.

''Greeks bearing gifts?'' she asked.

''I don't follow,'' he said, and then threw back his head and laughed. ''As if I ever did follow whatever it was that you were up to!''

''You come empty-handed,'' she explained. ''I told your daughter I was hungry.''

''Ah. That I can understand. I'll get you——''

''No,'' she interrupted. ''I want to get up and come downstairs. I want to see people and hear things.'' She threw back the blanket that covered her, and instantly regretted it. ''I don't seem to have very much clothing. Could you—please? My robe in the closet.''

He grinned, a sort of wolfish grin.

''And maybe you could go back downstairs and Maude could come up and help me?''

''Spoilsport.''

She glared at him.

''All right, all right. Don't lose your cool, lady. I'm going.''

Maude must have been standing just outside the door, as she and her father passed each other the child gave him a very wise and adult look, almost as if she were sticking her tongue out at him. And he didn't stray too far, either. No sooner had Maude helped Lucy put on her robe than he was back, offering his arm.

"The stairs are pretty steep. After all this to-do I think you need some help. In fact..." He swung her up in his arms and carried her down the stairs, depositing her in the deep captain's chair that was the set piece of the kitchen. "So there," he concluded.

"You're huffing and puffing," she said softly.

"What do you know about that? I'm mainly an office-type worker. Or perhaps I'd better amend that. I *was* mainly an office-type worker."

Lucy, who was out of breath herself, pondered. To ask or not to ask? As he'd carried her downstairs the warmth of him had invaded her. The imprint of his hand, just below the swell of her breast, would be with her forever. Or so she thought. So I *will* ask.

"You *were* an office-type worker."

"That's right."

"Meaning that you aren't any more?"

"The doctor said you could have broth for a day or so. How would you like your broth?"

"Hot and in a mug," she said. "And I'm not a great lover of broth. What I really need is a good steak. With mashed potatoes and the like."

"Broth," he said sternly. "Why pay the doctor those fantastic prices if you don't intend to follow his instructions?"

"Maybe because I'm broke and I don't intend to pay him anything at all. You'd better call him up and tell him I'm a charity patient. That'll cut down all this advice about broth. Now, about what you do for a living."

He got up from his chair and came around the table to where she was sitting. Those dark eyes were boring holes in her. Nervous, Lucy adjusted the bodice of her robe, and re-tied the belt that held it all together.

"That won't do you any good," he commented as he put one hand on her shoulder.

"I don't know what you're up to, Jim Proctor," she said. "But you'll kindly remember that your daughter is here in the house with us."

"Did anyone ever tell you that you talk too much?"

"What are you doing now?" Her voice went upscale from calm comment to a squeak of alarm.

"I'm trying to find your shut-off switch."

"You're a cruel man, Mr. Proctor. Maybe I won't marry you after all."

"More threats? Ah, now I see how it works." His head came down over her, brooded for a second, and then his lips sealed her mouth. For a second Lucy panicked and fought back. Only for a second. The contact of his mouth on hers sent little shivers up and down her spine. Unfair, she yelled at herself. Unfair advantage. But it was a lovely advantage, and she relaxed languidly and let it all happen. When finally he moved back an inch or two she gasped for breath, and sent commands through her whole nervous system, ordering surrender.

"What are you waiting for now?" Said breathlessly, as if she expected him to produce a knife and dispatch her.

"I'm waiting for the protest. The scream. The lecture. The diatribe."

She grinned up at him, and used a finger to brush the hair out of her eyes. "You've got the wrong girl. I enjoyed it. You won't get any diatribes from me. How about another sample?"

"Lucy, your broth is getting cold." Eagle-eyed Maude called her back to duty.

"Damn," he said.

"Tut-tut. Duty before pleasure." The reluctant arms let her go. She pulled back a little way and readjusted her robe, which by this time needed considerable adjustment. And then, to shut off the nagging, sipped at the broth and managed a gigantic sigh.

"What's that mean?" the little girl asked.

"That's a question," Lucy returned. "It means how do I get the lovely little lady to go outside and play so I can talk to her dad, man-to-man—oops, I mean man-to-woman style?"

"You mean I should butt out?"

"Exactly. How clever some of these modern phrases are."

"So I'm going." Maude was all smiles. She thought she knew what was in the works. In hardly a minute the pair of them inside could hear her wild yell as she ran up and down the beach, playing with a neighbor-hood dog.

"Now, then," she said, and turned to face him.

"You make that sound like the judge about to pass sentence."

"Well, you'll admit that we parted on pretty bad grounds, Mr. Proctor, and then all of a sudden you're back, all peaches and cream. A few words of explanation might not go amiss, as they used to say."

"Well, Your Honor, it was like this. I didn't mean to, but I fell in love with a girl in the neighborhood. But I really was a little scared about this marriage business. I had tried it before, and it was a dismal flop."

"That's a good start. Now, get to the important part."

"So I conceived this totally idiotic idea of marrying my sister-in-law. And then I decided that I shouldn't marry for my own needs, but rather for my daughter's. Which caused me to approach Lucastra Borden and demand that *she* marry me——"

"For your daughter's sake, of course."

"As you say. For my daughter's sake. And then it came to me that perhaps I could combine the two. Marry her for my own sake first, and then, as an afterthought, for my daughter's."

"That's a clever switch. Two for the price of one, so to speak."

"Well, not exactly. Because I found myself falling in love. Head over heels in love. And that's hardly the thing for a staid small-town banker."

"Ah. The bank. I knew the villain had to appear someplace. Do go on."

"Let me say something first, Lucy. I'm not a very bright man. The only way I've managed to get ahead was to fight and stomp and growl."

"I noticed that the first day we met," she said. "I thought you wanted to bite my head off, and I hate dominating men. Surely hate them."

Jim Proctor looked at her. Not a beauty, not at all, especially with her hair all disheveled, and the sleep sand still in the corners of her eyes. But she was a woman. All woman, every inch of her. And of all the round dozen things he could think of to do with this all woman, the one he might most easily get away with was to put his arm around her. He walked out to the living room, and sat down on the couch. She followed, but was hesitant about sharing with him.

Jim patted the space beside him. She debated the subject with herself for a moment, and then came. "Closer," he ordered.

She gave him a little dig. "I don't like dominant males. Especially those that give orders." But she moved anyway. So close that her thigh touched his. She was wearing thin silk; he was wrapped up in the typical businessman's uniform. I could have worn shorts, he told himself, and pounded his fist on the arm of the couch, a sort of self-punishment.

"That's no way to do." She picked up his bruised fist and cherished it against the softness of her breast. Jim instantly found his mood improving. By the mile, that improvement. What is she going to do next?

She tugged at the fingers of his fist, without the strength to unfold them. I'm no fool, Jim told himself, and relaxed his fingers. She folded them out flat in her lap, tugging and straightening them out.

"Why are you doing that?"

"Because I want to." She lifted his unfolded hand and placed it flat across her left breast. Without any instructions from him, the fingers closed into a rounded cup.

"You didn't even like me the first day we met," she mused.

"That was because you took Maude out of our environment—the space we had planned to control against any kind of threat. But that night I discovered that you wouldn't slay a mouse. And that you loved my daughter. And that you had the sexiest figure I've seen in many a day." His hand squeezed gently on the rounded mound within its control. Nothing in the world could be that soft, he told himself.

"So then you offered to marry me just to take care of Maude."

"Lord, wasn't that most stupid ploy you ever heard of? But it was the best I could think of at the moment. By that time I was head over teakettle, and everything I did was pointed toward getting you to the altar. You *are* going to marry me, aren't you?"

"I—haven't decided yet. Now, what is it that you've done in the past few days to change your way of life?"

"You mean outside of coming back for you? Somebody put Angie's death notice in the *Boston Globe*. You have no idea how fast a man can pack up."

"I'll bet half your stuff is still up in Boston. But I get the impression that you're waltzing, Mr. Proctor. Just what did you do that——?"

"I can't wait another minute," he said, and grabbed at her with both hands. She went willingly, tucking the top of her head just under his chin, watching as his hands wandered, sighing as he kissed her lips. All of which left her slightly out of breath, and wanting something more. She was driving herself frantic, trying to watch his every move. So naturally she missed the one that unbuttoned the top of her nightdress, and let the cool wind blow across her breasts. A moment later he was kneeling on the floor, and she was stretched out on the couch, and the sharp perfection of his teeth were nipping at her nipple.

Lucy went rigid, from head to toe, rigid. Tensions she had never dreamed of appeared in flashes, and were soothed lingeringly as his tongue replaced his finger. Her robe slipped off her shoulders, and she didn't care. Not until there was a massive knock on the back door, it opened, and Mr. Henderson walked in on them.

"Well, now," he said in his heavy rough voice. "Heard you was back, so I said, Herman, I said.

That's my Christian name. I was named after my uncle. A fine builder and horse thief in the old country. Well, I says to myself, the little lady must be sick to the death about that busted staircase in the back. Probably she's been climbing over it every day, cussin' the name of Henderson. So here I am, ready to finish it up. If you was wantin' it, of course?''

"Oh, yes, we need the steps," Lucy said weakly. Immediately on recognition, she had jumped up, and now stood behind Jim's back as she fumbled with her robe and nightgown. "Yes," she repeated. "As quickly as possible. And—Mr. Henderson. That check I gave you? Did you——?''

"Tuck it straight to the bank the first day," he drawled. "Been workin' at carpentry for nigh on to twenty-eight years. Got me an old proverb—trust anybody in the business. Starting on when you're comin' back from the bank.''

"Very funny, Mr. Henderson," Jim announced. "Yes, we want the steps fixed. Today, if possible. Can you start right away?''

"Just the kinda man I understand, little lady. Begin this minute, shall I?''

"This very minute," Lucy agreed. "If not sooner.''

The old man guffawed and slapped his pant leg. "Beats me," he announced as he started for the door. "Beats me how a little tyke like you can have all that gumption. Get straightened up with your banker feller, did you?''

"Yes, she seems to have." Jim had a very narrow little smile on his face. The kind of smile the tiger used just before it began to eat. Lucy backed away from him into a corner.

"Look," she implored him, "I didn't mean to do you out of your money. Not at first, that is. But then it seemed so easy that—well, I just didn't know when to say no! And now, I suppose, you'll want all your money back, and you'll drive off into the sunset again."

"Yes and no, lady." She could back no farther than the coffee table, and he was surrounding her with those firm arms. Not that I'm going to struggle *too* much, she told herself. In fact, she covered the last few inches under her own power. "Now, where was I?" he asked as he nibbled on the lobe of her ear.

"No, you don't." She managed to get both hands up against his chest, and pushed. He moved hardly an inch. "No more of that game until you tell me. Why aren't you angry that I tried to get money from your bank?"

"Nosy," he said, chuckling. "I'm not angry because I've spent the last four days up in Boston, selling out all my shares of stock."

"Then you're—you're broke?"

"Not exactly broke, but yes, in reduced circumstances. I figured I'd live off your income."

"Mine? For goodness' sake, I don't make enough money to keep Maude in socks. Schoolteachers, especially substitutes, don't make a great deal of money! Why did you sell the bank?''

"Because I figured it would always come between us. As it has in the past, love.''

"Ah." A bright thought flashed across her mobile face. With her hands behind her back—with fingers crossed—she stretched up on tiptoes and kissed his chin. Which was all she could reach at the moment. "Then I won't have to repay the loan on my house?''

"What?''

Lucy backed away, ready to duck. That wasn't the right question to be asking at the moment, apparently.

"Good Lord, no wonder a lot of banks are being closed! With people like you around! Good Lord.''

Her pixie face went all solemn. "I asked you a simple question, and I don't understand the answer.''

"The answer is as simple as the question,'' he said. The surprised look was gone from his face; smiles were the order of the day. "No, you don't have to repay the loan. In Massachusetts a husband is responsible for all his wife's debts. What do you think about that?''

"You mean—you——?''

"Don't giggle so much. You'll choke yourself to death. And that I can't allow. In later years I might want to do the choking myself. Yes, Lucastra, I have to pay off your loan.''

"Now that's the funniest thing I ever heard of,'' Lucy said between convulsions. "If all the wives in the world knew that, most of the men——''

"Would be broke, or bachelors. Now, where were we?"

"Right here, I think." She took that massive hand of his, kissed the palm, and set it in place again on her breast. Somehow her robe slipped again. Silk is always slippery, she defended her actions to herself. So it's not my fault, really. The straps of the nightgown came off next, slipping off her shoulders. He leaned down to encompass her breast again. The shock was instant. Waves of frustration swept over Lucy's previously unawakened body. His free hand came up behind her, resting on her hip, where the nightgown hung.

And the front door slammed open and Maude came into the entry hall, yelling in a loud voice. "Mom. Mom! I met Mrs. Winters as she was coming back from vacation and I said my new mom owns this house, and she said she always wanted to see over the inside of it and I said this is a fine time to do it, so here she is, and—— *Mom*? Mom?"

CHAPTER TEN

ON HER wedding day Lucastra found out how many friends she really had. The church was packed as she drove up to the double doors in the back seat of her future husband's Cadillac. Even Mr. Ledderman and his new wife were standing outside the door in the brilliant sun.

The bride was traditionally dressed. A long white gown of clinging silk, with a short train and a pair of cotton petticoats. A high mandarin collar, to which was pinned a beautiful brooch loaned by Mrs. Winters. A blue garter on one thigh, the old watch her father had given her so many years ago on her wrist, and a lovely new friendship ring sparkling on her right hand. A small half veil, and a little coronet of gold completed the ensemble. Real gold, Jim had told her, and she'd almost choked! As she walked she rustled. And smiled, because the sound was fairylike, and she had loved the old stories in her grandmother's story book.

Four days until the end of August, she told herself as she climbed out of the car with Mr. Henderson's assistance. Seven days until the start of school. How in the world are we going to live on *my* income?

Trying to get Jim to talk about the subject was like trying to climb Mount Everest barefoot. "Not to worry," he kept saying. "Things are bound to turn out all right!" And then he would raise his head just a little bit to stare down at her, and he would chuckle.

A most infuriating man. But a hardworking girl could make something out of him yet, if she put her mind to it! And then I have to get him to shave more often, she thought. Since he'd stopped being a banker he seemed to think that shaving once a week was good enough. This man certainly had to be taken in hand. And I'm the girl to do it! Or am I?

"Watch the step." Mr. Henderson was all solicitude, dressed to the nines, with a floppy black tie that looked like a pair of wings. But he knew the marrying business, as he told her. "Shoveled off four daughters of my own, I have, and a niece of my brother's. And not a one of them as cute as you, lady."

So, since she knew that was a fabulous feat, she congratulated him and they walked into the vestibule. The organ was playing Bach. A prelude, her hazy mind told her, but there was no way she could remember which one. The minister stood at the end of the central aisle, and her little flower girl was dancing up and down madly.

"What's the trouble, Maude?"

"I gotta go, and they won't let me."

"Go. Go quickly." Lucy signaled for one of her four bridesmaids to guard the trail. The Reverend Falson, who had seen many catastrophes before, nodded, made some obscure signal to the organist, and eventually the flower girl came back—flustered, rosy cheeked from embarrassment, but back.

"Ready?" Maude nodded. Mr. Henderson gave some signal, the Reverend Falson relayed something to the organ loft, and the parade began. Everything went just as if they had never rehearsed, which they hadn't. The organ swelled triumphantly, Mr. Henderson put her hand under his arm and gave it a little pat, and Lucy Borden went off on her maiden cruise.

It was hard to keep a straight face. She knew practically everyone in the church, but a bride should never stop to chat on her processional walk. Face straight ahead, she acknowledged close friends with a fractional wink, and, though she never had believed it would happen, she and Mr. Henderson came to the altar without incident. Somehow her hand was transferred to Jim's, Mr. Henderson lifted her veil, kissed her himself, and faded off into the pews.

"Dearly beloved," Reverend Falson began in his fine deep voice, and Lucy, looking at Jim out of the corner of her eye, lost all contact with reality. Words rolled over her head without comprehension until the good minister came to that part about, "Alexander James, wilt thou have this woman to thy wedded wife…?" Lucy almost swallowed her bubble gum, and stared at the stranger beside her. Alexander? Whatever happened to Jimbo? She was still wrestling with *that* problem when the minister said, "I pronounce that

they be man and wife together. Kiss the bride, Jimbo."
So it must be all right if the man of God said so, and
whoever the rascal was, when he kissed her she knew
it was Jimbo himself, and she had come home.

"Now?" Maude asked when they got out to the
cars.

"Now," her father said. The little girl ran back to
stand at the front of the crowd, and Lucy tossed her
bouquet directly to Maude. "Good catch," they both
told her when she came running back to the car, flowers in hand.

"And that means I'm going to be the next one to
marry?"

"But don't hurry it," Jim cautioned her. "Your
mother and I could use a baby-sitter for a while."

"Tonight?"

"Not quite that soon," Lucy said, blushing. "He
means after a time. Someday. Maybe."

"Next year at this time," Jim insisted, and Lucy
ducked her head to hide the blush. Really, she
thought, this man has *got* to be taken in hand. But a
girl doesn't have to assert herself on the very first day
of her wedded life.

The reception was held on the beach between the
two houses. There were a large number of bottles, two
casks of beer, and a line of volunteer nondrinkers to
get them all home. Not to mention the two volunteers
from the police department, the barbecued burgers
and the hot dogs. And by that time it was coming on
dark, the beach was filled with shadows, and the three

Proctors walked up to the veranda of the big house.
Maude held the door, and Jim carried the bride across
the threshold, and then put on a make-believe act,
panting and gasping for breath.

"Well, that was nice—Mom," the little girl said
between yawns. "I wanna stay up to see *Hunter* now."

"The party's over," her new mother said. "No
daughter of mine is going to sit up until all hours of
the night to watch mayhem on television. Your dad
and I are going to bed . . ." And in a whisper, "Stop
that, Jim. Be patient!"

"Aw, gee!"

"That's enough, girl. Your mother told you to
scoot. You scoot."

The precocious little girl stuck her tongue out at
them both, giggled like crazy, and ran for the stairs
and her bedroom.

"Shall we?" Lucy's husband murmured.

"Race you," his bride said as she hitched up her
long skirts and raced for the master bedroom. It was
a dead heat. After he had introduced her to woman-
hood they lay exhausted and totally nude atop the
sheets, when someone knocked at their door.

"Oh, no," he groaned, "not here too."

"Maude?" Lucy asked.

"I can't get to sleep," the child called as she started
to open the door. There was a flurry of action inside
the bedroom. Jim managed to find his pajamas; Lucy
struggled to find her filmy nightgown, and when she
did it was ripped.

The child was in the room. Lucy ducked beneath the sheet, leaving Jim to face the music.

"Mom? Can I come in your bed with you?"

"If you say yes," he hissed at his new wife, "I'll break your head!"

"Not tonight dear. Daddy's not feeling well. But he'll come back to your bed with you and tell you a story. Won't you, dear?"

"I'll get you," he muttered as he slipped out of bed.

"I hope so," she called after him. And to her surprise he did.

The next morning came early, and for once he had shown great skill. When they opened their eyes at six o'clock he had locked the bedroom door, and Maude, after knocking what seemed like endless times, had to paddle downstairs to have breakfast with Mrs. Winters.

"I don't see why they gotta sleep in late," the child complained.

"It happens a lot with newlyweds," Mrs. Winters assured her. "Just be patient. They'll be along."

And so they did, shortly after noontime.

They had brunch out on the beach, dressed in bathing suits. "You need a bikini," he said.

"You need another cup of coffee," she returned. "Maude, did you want some coffee?"

The invitation was too much to miss. The child came to them, all smiles, and they ate as if they had

had nothing for a week. "And now there are a couple of things we have to talk about," Jim Proctor said.

"First of all, about the bank. I'd almost become married to that damn institution. When I learned about your—loan—I became so angry that I could have eaten wallpaper. So I ran away from it all, to give myself a chance to think. Well, what I thought is that I would have to give up being a banker if I wanted to have you. I sold off all my shares in the bank and— would you know?—we are fifteen dollars short of being millionaires. Now, after a while I'm going to go back to law school, and be a lawyer. But before I do that we three of us are going on a honeymoon."

"Me too?" Maude asked.

"You too," he said, giving her hand a little squeeze.

"And are we poor females to be told *where* we're going?"

"No reason why not. I took a big map last week and found a hundred places we ought to go to, so, in order to get everything in, we're going to take a trip around the world. Now don't everyone shout in glee about my choice! We're going to spend our first week in Washington, and your mother is going to take you on all the guided tours of the city while I testify in front of the senate banking committee. For some reason they seem to think that, although I'm out of the banking business, I still might think of a thing or two of importance to say."

"Aw, give us a break," his daughter said, breathless.

"Holy cow," his bride remarked. "Around the world? What on earth are we going to live on?"

"Your mother is Mrs. Practical Pig," Jim told his daughter. "Everything dotted and signed over. Well, Mrs. Proctor, I just told you, didn't I, that we are fifteen dollars short of being millionaires?"

"Great," Lucy said. "I know this bank where we could easily borrow fifteen dollars. Maybe even twenty!"

"Oh, no, you don't," he said, grabbing both her little hands. "You, lady, are finished with the banking business. Besides, do you remember when Angie Moore made you a gift of all those papers and things in her cupboard? She left you her widow's mite. Remember?"

"What's that mean?" Maude insisted.

"It's a story from the Bible," her father said. "The widow, who had only one mite to her name. That's the smallest coin they had back in those days. She came up to the temple, walked by all the rich people who were talking to each other, and she threw her mite into the collection box, giving everything she had to God. And that's what Angie did. Only it's not a mite any more, love. When the bank clerks got through totaling your complete inheritance it came to four million dollars. Not counting the fifty thousand in Confederate dollars, which, I suppose, aren't tradeable on the open market."

"I—good Lord, I had forgotten," Lucy murmured. "Dear Angie. But her widow's mite was not money, it was love. She left us all the example of how one can be happy and still sacrifice for the sake of others. You know, she wanted so much for me to marry you, Alexander."

"Me too. So, you see, we don't have to live on your salary. In fact, I told the school principal at the wedding that you wouldn't be back. And don't you ever call me Alexander in public," he corrected her. "Yes, dear Angie, and dear Lucy."

"And dear me," Maude concluded. "Ain't you guys gonna swim?"

"I don't think so," Lucy said. "Your father and I have some things to talk over, and then I think we need a nap. You go and stay with Mrs. Winters, and we'll see you for supper."

"I don't understand," Maude complained the next day. "You guys have been sleepin' practically all day yesterday, and half the day today. And you're still tired! I think they need some vitamin pills, Mrs. Winters."

"You may be right," the housekeeper said. And then, to Jim, "You have the urn?"

"Yes, and the seaplane is just coming in down there now. Come on, Maude."

"Come on where, for goodness' sakes?"

"You and I and your mother are going to go for an airplane ride, and say goodbye to Angie."

"To Angie? But she's—gone."

"Yes, but she'll be there to say goodbye to us, just the same. Get a sweater. It will be cold up there in the plane."

The seaplane landed in the millpond calm of the harbor, and taxied up to the end of the jetty by the Proctor house. The pilot helped them in, Jim in the front seat, and Lucy and Maude side by side on the back bench, strapped in. It took but minutes for the pilot to get clearance to take off. He swept inland around to route six, and then came out over the harbor, flaps down, and maintaining just enough speed to stay aloft.

Jim Proctor opened the sliding window in the door beside him, and at the pilot's command he tilted the urn and the ashes floated gently out on the breeze and began to scatter.

"Ashes to ashes," Lucy murmured, and there was a tear in her eye. "Goodbye, Angie Moore, God rest you." And then she turned to Maude, because in Lucastra Proctor's world there was always a moral to every story. "I was a baby when my real mother died," she said. "My grandmother took care of me for many years, and then, after she passed on, Angie became my second mother. She was very good to me."

"And look at me," Maude said excitedly. "My mother died when I was young, and now I've got you for a second mother. Wow! Am I gonna have it made for a long time!"

Lucy, who had never quite seen things that way, worked up a wonderful smile and wiped the tear trying to steal down her cheek as she exchanged a glance with her husband.

"G'bye, Angie," Maude said. "We'll see you in heaven."

"Well, wasn't that a nice thing to say?" Lucy commented. "I—perhaps we will. Let's go home, Jim. Today is the first day of the rest of our lives."

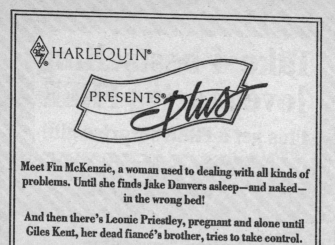

Take 4 bestselling love stories FREE

Plus get a FREE surprise gift!

Special Limited-time Offer

Mail to Harlequin Reader Service®

3010 Walden Avenue
P.O. Box 1867
Buffalo, N.Y. 14269-1867

YES! Please send me 4 free Harlequin Presents® novels and my free surprise gift. Then send me 6 brand-new novels every month, which I will receive months before they appear in bookstores. Bill me at the low price of $2.24 each plus 25¢ delivery and applicable sales tax, if any*. That's the complete price and—compared to the cover prices of $2.99 each—quite a bargain! I understand that accepting the books and gift places me under no obligation ever to buy any books. I can always return a shipment and cancel at any time. Even if I never buy another book from Harlequin, the 4 free books and the surprise gift are mine to keep forever.

106 BPA AJJA

Name	(PLEASE PRINT)
Address	Apt. No.
City	State	Zip

This offer is limited to one order per household and not valid to present Harlequin Presents® subscribers. *Terms and prices are subject to change without notice. Sales tax applicable in N.Y.

Calloway Corners

In September, Harlequin is proud to bring readers four involving, romantic stories about the Calloway sisters, set in Calloway Corners, Louisiana. Written by four of Harlequin's most popular and award-winning authors, you'll be enchanted by these sisters and the men they love!

MARIAH by Sandra Canfield
JO by Tracy Hughes
TESS by Katherine Burton
EDEN by Penny Richards

As an added bonus, you can enter a sweepstakes contest to win a trip to Calloway Corners, and meet all four authors. Watch for details in all Calloway Corners books in September.

HARLEQUIN CELEBRATES
THE SEASON OF SHARING
AND FAMILY WITH

Friends, Families, Lovers

Harlequin introduces the latest member in its family of seasonal collections. Following in the footsteps of the popular *My Valentine, Just Married* and *Harlequin Historical Christmas Stories*, we are proud to present FRIENDS, FAMILIES, LOVERS. A collection of three new contemporary romance stories about America at its best, about welcoming others into the circle of love.... Stories to warm your heart ...

By three leading romance authors:

KATHLEEN EAGLE
SANDRA KITT
RUTH JEAN DALE

Available in October, wherever
Harlequin books are sold.

Fifty red-blooded, white-hot, true-blue hunks from every
State in the Union!

Beginning in May, look for MEN MADE IN AMERICA!
Written by some of our most popular authors, these
stories feature fifty of the strongest, sexiest men, each
from a different state in the union!

Two titles available every other month at your favorite
retail outlet.

In September, look for:

DECEPTIONS by Annette Broadrick (California)
STORMWALKER by Dallas Schulze (Colorado)

In November, look for:

STRAIGHT FROM THE HEART by Barbara Delinsky
(Connecticut)
AUTHOR'S CHOICE by Elizabeth August (Delaware)

You won't be able to resist MEN MADE IN AMERICA!